BOW

'The questi
about the room, leaving significant footprints of slush on his host's thick pile, 'what brings Smirnov back to these parts? I grant you, he's not the biggest fish in the Kremlin's pond; but he's definitely a man for troubled waters — pretty murky and dangerous waters at that.'

'He's clearly a card they play with care and deliberation. As you say we haven't heard a whisper of him since Goodwood 1959.'

'But the thing that worries me — and I can assure you it's worrying the Prime Minister — is what the hell is this nasty little killer doing at Worcester County Cricket Ground during the Derbyshire match of all insane things? Are you listening, James?'

Still cradling his balloon glass on his knee, his head sunk into the upturned collar of his old MCC dressing gown like an exhausted tortoise, James Ball was snoring.

Also in Arrow by Allen Synge

TALES FROM FAR PAVILIONS (editor, with Leo Cooper)

BOWLER, BATSMAN, SPY

Allen Synge

ARROW BOOKS

Arrow Books Limited
62–65 Chandos Place, London WC2N 4NW

An imprint of Century Hutchinson Ltd

London Melbourne Sydney Auckland
Johannesburg and agencies throughout
the world

First published by
George Weidenfeld & Nicolson Limited 1985

Arrow edition 1986

Printed and bound in Great Britain by
Anchor Brendon Limited, Tiptree, Essex

ISBN 0 09 944170 5

Dedication

This book is dedicated to my son, Timothy Auchmuty Synge. He has been a valued consultant on the work and I am particularly indebted to him for his advice on the selection of England's team for the disastrous Headingley Test.

At the same time I wish to touch my cap in salute to that master of espionage fiction, John le Carré.

A.S.

Note:

The action of this book takes place sometime in the near past when the national game was reaching crisis point.

CONTENTS

PROLOGUE

He was met by an official limousine at Kazan station and driven in silence through the moist streets to his appointment at Dzerzhinsky Square. It was April in Moscow and the weather was a mirror of I. Smirnov's mood. Cold and drear with just a suggestion of hopeful sunlight somewhere behind the smudgy clouds. However this sense of expectation, such as it was, drained away as the car pulled up at the hunk of masonry called the Marshal Voroshilov Buildings. But then nobody walks into a KGB office complex with a spring in his step, even when, as was Smirnov's case, he has been recalled from years of thankless duty on the borders of China.

A single-eyed commissionaire, old enough to have lost the other in the Second World War, directed him to Briefing Room 13. At least Smirnov was relieved it was a room and not a cell.

Red and gold epaulettes and bulging khaki tunics suggested this was to be no minor bureaucratic affair. And there were other men in nondescript pin-stripes and serge whom Smirnov sensed could be at least as powerful. Did he not recognize among their mirthless faces the celebrated English defector, KGB General Field? But who was this white-haired eccentric making splay-footed steps towards the podium? He looked like an intellectual dissident fresh from forty years hard labour in the Gulag. But apparently this was a false impression. He was being introduced, in nearly reverential tones, as Comrade Professor Nikitin Yakov, Section Manager of the KGB's Statistical

Department, and certainly there was an air of authority in the way in which he signalled to the projectionist.

An ancient building, such as could only be found undemolished in Russia in the outskirts of Leningrad or the backwaters of Odessa, was flashed on the screen.

'The Marylebone County Cricket Club,' Comrade Professor Yakov announced, 'colloquially known to Englishmen as "the Lords" – the heart and brain of the United Kingdom's cricket power.'

'What please is cricket?' asked some moon-faced novice at the back of the briefing room.

Professor Yakov killed him with a stare. 'Cricket, as comrades will learn if they are good enough to give me their full concentration, is the most reliable measurement we have of Britain's economic and military capability. You will see that I have statistics to prove my thesis.'

A picture of a depraved couple of young Westerners copulating openly on a dance floor was thrown up on the screen behind Yakov's silvery hairs.

'This is the impression many of us will have of England,' said the Comrade Professor. 'A post-imperialist nation of declining military power becoming increasingly impoverished in moral authority.'

A picture of English paratroopers in a Belfast or a Port Stanley street replaced the young fornicators.

'However in certain periods during the Post-War years, which I will demonstrate to be cyclical, this England has proved it is still able to act with virility and purpose. . . .'

Pictures of the peasant Queen and the insane aristocrat Thatcher supplant the para-fascists.

' . . . to such a degree,' opined the Comrade Professor, 'that it would still be prudent to make the social demoralization of England a matter of priority after the United States.'

Red and gold epaulettes and a bulging khaki tunic lumbered to their feet.

'Comrade Professor, I am sure comrades are aware of the strategic importance of the United Kingdom to the hostile

Western Alliance. You will be kind enough to confine yourself to the presentation of statistics.'

Yakov smiled at him like some Soviet scientist denied the privilege of collecting his Nobel Prize and gave an almost contemptuous flick of the fingers.

A bearded pensioner in an English schoolboy's cap now dominated the screen. He was holding an instrument which Smirnov identified as a type of horticultural instrument, but was shortly able to recognize, only too well, as another dreaded cricket bat. In the same way that those crude trouser reinforcements would soon become all too familiar to him as 'pads'.

'The Doctor W.G. Grace,' snarled Yakov, 'England's greatest batterman – at least until the hay days of Hobbs, J. B. and Compton, D. C. S.

'This Doctor represents the high tide of English cricket achievement,' proclaimed the arrogant egg-head. 'It is significant to note that the spectacular career of Doctor W.G. corresponds precisely with England's most assured successes as an Imperialist power. Let me give you an example. In the year in which this giant achieves the astonishing aggregate of 48,000 runs in all matches, expansionist forces under Marshal Kitchener overthrow the legitimate Patriotic People's Republic of the Mahdi and establish British Middle Eastern domination as far south as Khartoum.

'Let us now turn to more recent developments in this peculiarly English game, all the time bearing in mind the connection I have identified between English achievements and failures on the cricket fields and those obtained on the wider geopolitical map.'

A forest of meaningless figures is flashed onto the screen.

'You are looking at the team averages of England's disastrous cricket engagements with Australia in the winter of 1920–1. Demoralized by the losses sustained in the Imperialist Kaiser War and the ruinous Churchillist intervention into our Revolution on behalf of the Whiteist jackals, this expedition is destined to lose a remarkable total of five Tests against the traditional Australian enemy, thus abjectly surrendering the mystical "Ash

Can" so dearly purchased by Mr P. F. Warner-Stand's tourists in the golden sunset of British global power in the winter of 1911–12.

'Look particularly at the comparatively disappointing Test battering average of Hobbs, J. B. and of Wooley, F. E. And consider the punishment meted out by Armstrong and his fellow Australian battermen as detailed in the bowling figures of the unhappy Captain, Mr J. W. T. Douglas.

'You will please now to pay attention to a contrasting set of statistics,' continued the white-haired pelican of a man, fastening his demented eyes on Smirnov in the act of reaching for his hip flask. 'The year is 1926. A Capitalist-fascist administration under First Minister Baldwin has recently crushed the Socialist-proletarian General Strike. England is beginning to flex again its old Imperialist revanchist muscles, and we see this is immediately reflected in the scores completed for the Fifth Test Match at the Oval of Surrey where England under the Captaincy of Mr A. P. F. Chapman repossessed the coveted "Ash Can". You will be so good as to note that even the aged Rhodes W. is sufficiently re-invigorated to return in the second innings bowling figures of four wickets for 44 runners.'

The statistics and the commentary now accelerated into a blinding collage of figures accompanied by shrill, hectoring, near incomprehensible words.

'See how the collapse of the British economy under the working-class turncoat MacDonald R. in the season of 1930 is discernible, with the certainty of a seismograph, in the disappointing scores achieved by the England cricketers against W. M. Woodful's Australian tourists that summer. . . .

'. . . consider now the equations of the season of 1953. A new Queen, the surmounting of Everest, the victory of the Jockey Club darling Richards G. in the Derby horse races – all contribute to a rekindling of aggressive imperialism sufficient to obtain for Sir Hutton, Len's, English professionals a victory over Australia by a margin of seven wicketers and the repossession after nineteen years of economic stagnation, appeasement and military humiliation of the talismatic "Ash Can".

'. . . 1957. The impact of the Suez fiasco is not immediately discernible in the performance of Mr P. B. Ash-May's Englanders who record a four to zero victory over an enfeebled West Indies. However the long term effects of this disaster can be measured in Ash-May's abortive defence of the "Ash Can" in the Australian season of 1958–9. So much so that you will note, if you consult the Wisden reference book, that the battermen Milton C. A., Mr P. E. Richardson and Watson W. are not again to enjoy the confidence of the Committee for Selection.'

A frantic coda of colour graphs finally bombarded the screen.

'Up to the most recent seasons,' screamed the Comrade Professor, 'we are able to observe this extraordinary resemblance between England's cricketering and socio-economic performance. You are looking at the graphs for the 1970s. You will see that the green line representing the fortunes of England's Test team elite conforms almost exactly to the up and down movements of the orange line representing Capitalist-Imperialist national moods, the blue line representing the House of Commons strength of the Conservative Party and the red line which measures the performance of the pound sterling against the US dollar.'

Then with a State actor's sense of timing Yakov slowly helped himself to a glass of water. Possibly it was laced with vodka, but Smirnov doubted it.

'These statistics,' the Professor licked his lips, 'demonstrate beyond all doubt that the socio-military-economic gradients we have charted have a direct influence on the aggregates achieved by the national cricket elevens.

'Now,' he crowed, fixing Smirnov with a stare of such intensity as to freeze the hip flask on his lips, 'let us examine the logical antitheses of my deductions. If socio-economic-paramilitary factors can be demonstrated to condition the health of this English cricket game, is it not reasonable to assume that a lethal injection into the English cricketering body would have a correspondingly mortal effect on the nation's wider capability? Let me encapsulate my thesis in a sentence:

"undermine the cricket of England and you destroy England itself!"'

In Smirnov's view this should have been Comrade Professor Yakov's final bow. He fully expected to see the podium surrounded by uniformed men – fully expected to see this overwrought scholar dragged away for another corrective spell in a suitable insane asylum.

Obviously he had seriously misjudged the new mood prevailing in the upper strata of his occasional employers. A sallow face from the ranks of the pin-stripe and serge suits had walked to the podium. He was thanking this maniac Yakov in the most effusive terms for his inspiring presentation. He went so far as to insist that his fevered findings could produce a sensational shift in the balance of world power. Worst of all, his beetle brows had finally come to rest on Smirnov. 'There will be comrades here this morning,' he said with heavy emphasis, 'who will know how to exploit the profound opportunities Comrade Professor Yakov's revolutionary statistics have created for us.'

This briefly was how I. Smirnov, a semi-disgraced KGB agent, now restored to something like full pay, was to be seen retching from the railings of the Hook-Harwich ferry into a mucus-green sea. And later to be observed shivering on the mostly deserted benches of the Worcestershire County Cricket Ground.

1

ST JOHN'S WOOD AWAKENING

The luminous bedside clock gleamed the intelligence that the time was 2.17 a.m. Too late for a political canvasser. Too early for the milkman, or one of those half-embarrassed, half-defiant returns by Jan.

Besides, the caller was hammering on the door like Vulcan. Neither the milkman nor Jan, even in her most contrite moods, ever hammered like that. James Ball, 'Bally' to his very few intimates, got out of bed with a sigh, put on an old MCC dressing gown and shuffled downstairs towards his buckling front door. In the dim passage light he looked not unlike Alec Guinness, dressed for his part in the *Star Wars* motion picture spectacular.

The caller was Hector Bootle of the Prime Minister's Security Adviser's Office. 'I'm sorry to break in on your domestic bliss, James,' he briefly apologized, 'but it is damned important.'

'It's all right,' Bally smiled self-deprecatingly, 'Jan is, as it were, playing away tonight.'

'Does that woman ever play anywhere else?' Hector Bootle boomed. 'Look James. One day when there isn't some ghastly flap on, you and I ought to go somewhere like Leeds or Trent Bridge and get completely smashed. Then perhaps you'll tell me what it is about bloody wives that makes them want to run away all the time. Mine left me yesterday – for Australia!'

'Hector, I hope you didn't wake me up in the middle of the

night to tell me about your marital tragedies,' Bally smiled wanly.

'I'm afraid it's rather more serious than that – look, exactly how much do you know about cricket?'

How much did he know about cricket? Bally repeated the question to himself with a flicker of a grin. He could have been patronizing. He could have reminded Bootle that he could recite every county championship winner from 1900 to 1965 by heart. He could have played the advantage of age by pointing out that he had seen Hobbs' square cut, Duleep's leg-glide, Wooley's plangent cover drives, was even senior enough to have been in a position to admire C. P. Meade's stolid defence.

If he had been a proud man, he could, of course, have invited Hector Bootle to come with him down the years to a certain afternoon at Lord's in the summer of 1931 and there pointed out to him a young man in spectacles nervously patrolling the square leg boundary under the light blue cap of Cambridge. With his quiet smile he could have indicated a scoreboard which would have shown Oxford well advanced into a record stand as the Cambridge spearhead of Farnes, Brown and Hazelrigg was mercilessly blunted. Finally he could have given Hector a discreet nudge as the battered ball was thrown despairingly to the nervous young man on the square leg boundary, and suggested he watched closely as the youth's feet stuttered to the crease and a gentle leg break rolled into the Oxford-blue sky – then rebounded from an over-eager crack from a Princely bat.

The Nawab of Pataudi c Kemp-Welch b Ball 238.

'How's that for cricket know-how?' Bally could, if he had been an arrogant man, have cried at his nocturnal visitor.

But then not all his experience of cricket could be described as a matter for pride. Cricket, if the truth was to be told, had also been a cause of distress and shame – white flannels, of course, being irresistible to Jan.

It had started with the Australian Tour of 1948. Or was it '38? In the early days her lies had been successful enough to permit of some vagueness as to dates and grounds. Later her infidelities were to become as precise as Wisden. Certainly there could be no vagueness about the date when the realization was forced upon Bally that he was married to a nymphomaniac.

Monday, 23 June 1948. Hutton c Johnson b Lindwall 13, Washbrook c Tallon b Toshack 37, Edrich c Johnson b Toshack 2 . . . England all out for a mournful 186 . . . victory for Bradman's implacable Australians by a gruesome margin of 499 runs. With bowed shoulders he had drifted back to the flat like a man in a bad dream and poured himself a stiff Courvoisier 6-star, notwithstanding the fact that every drop of the stuff had to be smuggled in by diplomatic bag in those days of austerity. It was then that he was confronted with evidence which even the most complaisant husband could not hope to ignore. An Australian cricket cap was perched at a rakish angle on his Dresden china cabinet. Seconds later he would discover on the stairs to the marriage bedroom a pair of boots which only hours before had helped to tread England underfoot.

So many seasons ago and still it hurt, despite all the subsequent betrayals. The springbok, the silver fern of New Zealand, the star of Pakistan, the emblematic palm and shore of the West Indies – in the fullness of time the regalia of all the Test-playing nations would be found draped around Bally's furniture.

It was easy to be censorious of Jan. But wasn't it possible that the initial fault had been his? His thoughtlessness and obstinacy in insisting they lived in St John's Wood?

The whole truth was that James Ball knew a great deal more than he cared to confess about the game of cricket, which was why he answered Hector Bootle's question with a modest 'I know a little. Why do you ask?'

'I've forgotten,' said Bootle. In fairness to the distraught official it had been a long time since he had asked the question. 'Ah yes, cricket, or more to the point a game of roulette – Russian Roulette! Dangerous for them. Potentially catastrophic for us. Smirnov is back in Britain.'

'Smirnov I. Special attaché for culture and sport. Diplomatic privileges withdrawn 23 July 1959,' James Ball quoted from his near computer-like memory. 'Deportation order confirmed 25 July 1959. A matter of some horseplay at Goodwood.'

'Exactly,' sighed Hector Bootle. 'Incidentally, it's snowing out here; is there any chance I could come in and have a glass of brandy – or at least a cup of Nescafé?'

'What proof have you got that Smirnov, the "horse doctor", is back in business?' Bally smiled ambiguously as he poured whistling hot water onto a teaspoon of granules.

'One of our people spotted him at Worcester Cricket Ground.'

'Who were they playing?' Bally enquired over the Nescafé spoon.

'Derbyshire: but the point is . . . .'

'I didn't know our friend was that keen on cricket,' Bally mused, pouring himself a stiff Courvoisier.

The old pro let the golden fire make a slow tour of his palate's outfield. 'Have you thought of talking to MI5 about this?' he asked at length.

'Good God no! Surely, James, you know as well as I do, you don't go near the boys at the "Oval" with anything more vital to the national interest than a missing cat.'

'A lovely batting strip the Oval,' Bally mused obtusely.

'Wake up James. You know it's bloody well honeycombed with moles!'

'Couldn't this be a job for Harry Grimaldi and his "Pitch Rollers"?' suggested the older man after another lingering sip.

Bootle shook his head vigorously. 'Too obvious and too messy! No, this assignment needs a certain delicacy, a certain finesse, a kind of *je ne sais quoi* – look I suppose I couldn't have a slug of that brandy, could I?'

'Or Bill Travers and his "Streakers"?' Bally superimposed another question.

'Too obvious and too risky,' Bootle grabbed the brandy bottle and slurped a shot into his Nescafé mug. 'No, try as we will I'm afraid we can find no alternative but to fall back on you James, you mean old bastard.'

'I'm old, I'm tired and I'm on an index-linked pension,' the doyen of spycatchers protested wearily.

'The question is, James,' Bootle began to pace about the room, leaving significant footprints of slush on his host's thick pile, 'what brings Smirnov back to these parts? I grant you, he's not the biggest fish in the Kremlin's pond; but he's definitely a man for troubled waters – pretty murky and dangerous waters at that.'

'He's clearly a card they play with care and deliberation. As you say we haven't heard a whisper of him since Goodwood 1959.'

'But the thing that worries me – and I can assure you it's worrying the Prime Minister – is what the hell is this nasty little killer doing at Worcester County Cricket Ground during the Derbyshire match of all insane things? Are you listening, James?'

Still cradling his balloon glass on his knee, his head sunk into the upturned collar of his old MCC dressing gown like an exhausted tortoise, James Ball was snoring.

2

ALBANY TRANSCRIPT

Sir Evelyn Lilliwhite, Director General of the Security Services, choked over his Mumm Champagne and began to gargle with the expensive stuff as if it were mouthwash.

'The dossier on the England cricket team!' he finally spluttered, 'Your friends in Moscow must be out of their tiny little minds!'

'Believe me, we are quite serious.' Smirnov leaned forward uncomfortably in the chintz-covered Louis Quinze. 'It is a matter of the utmost priority.' A clot of half-melted ice slipped from the Russian's shoe. It had been snowing at Worcester and also at Paddington.

'Well you've come to the wrong person!' Sir Evelyn shrilled. 'I don't know anything about the dreary English cricket team. I couldn't care less about those frightful little men in crash helmets and, frankly, I'm far from curious to know what they keep under those obscene plastic cod-pieces. If you want to know, I detest cricket. At my prep school I positively loathed being beaten with a cricket stump, merely because I was supposed to have dropped somebody called Colin Cowshot. To be perfectly candid it was sodding cricket that drove me into the arms of you people. Well how would you like to be put in a cage – or do they call it a net? It's so long ago and I can't bear to remember – stood up, anyway, against the stumps while ferocious bullies tried to knock one's head off. Oh, I know you can be a little rough with your dissidents, but this was torture, sheer, unadulterated torture! I don't want to think about the beastly game!'

'Comrade Sir Lilliwhite,' Smirnov answered earnestly. 'You must appreciate that in Moscow we have not your sources of information about this game and its prominent English players. The Controller is looking to your Service to provide this data for the Party. For instance,' Smirnov produced a crumpled sheet of notes, 'the Controller is confidently expecting that you will be able to supply us with a forecast of the names that will most likely to be selected for the First Test Match at the Old Trafford, for possible liquidation.'

'I wish you'd strangle every cricketer in creation,' Sir Evelyn hissed as he reached nervously for the ice bucket. 'And those dreadful commentators too, while you're about it! Believe me they make my summer an absolute misery. You don't hear a note of good music while those excruciating bores are hogging the air time. Not a whisper of my dear Mahler.'

'Ah Robin Marler, the former Sussex Turner and leading cricket authority for *The Sunday Times*,' Smirnov exclaimed with a sudden smile of pride in his amazing conjuring trick of memory. 'Could this Marler not be useful to us in our researches?'

'I'm talking about *the* Mahler, ducky!'

'I have names about which I shall be requiring intimate details,' the Russian nevertheless persisted. 'This Robert Taylor, for instance, what are his character defects? Where is he vulnerable? The Controller will require to know. This Gower, David. We understand he bats only with the left hand. Has he other peculiarities? This Christopher Tavaritch? Has he perhaps grandparents and relations in the Soviet Union to whom pressure could be applied? How easy would it be to compromise this Derek Randall?'

'Listen,' said the Director General of the Security Services, 'I've got a sweet little Wing Commander down in Cheltenham who's just longing to divulge. Now he *would* be someone worth talking to. He's responsible for a perfectly enormous data bank containing just about everything you still don't know about our advanced early warning systems. Why don't you let me fix up a meeting? You'd find it so much more rewarding than this pointless cricket exercise – and he's a lot of fun, I mean socially.'

Smirnov was inclined to agree with the distinguished British mole. As the elegant knight deftly squeezed open another bottle of Mumm's and splashed a generous measure into his glass, Smirnov was tempted to unbutton his greatcoat and confide his fears that the KGB had allowed themselves to be blinded by an insane science. He wanted to tell Sir Evelyn all about the lunatic Professor Yakov and the perverse video presentation which had launched him on his desperate mission. However, he had been out in the cold for the last twenty-five years – observing troop movements on the Russo-Chinese border on half pay and no expenses. He had a vested interest in obeying his orders scrupulously. His orders were to obtain the maximum co-operation of MI5. He dutifully tried another tack.

'Comrade Sir Lilliwhite, it has not escaped our attention in Moscow that the cover name for your operation is the "Oval", nor are we ignorant of the fact that the Kensington Oval is the traditional venue of your Fifth Test Matches. Surely does not this indicate some interest and knowledge of cricket among your department?'

'Grow up darling,' Sir Evelyn chided. 'Didn't they teach you that the whole point of a cover name is that it's perfectly pointless? Besides everyone knows we're really based in Piccadilly Circus.'

'Sir Lilliwhite,' reluctantly Smirnov set down his champagne glass on a Hepplewhite occasional table, 'I must insist that you are more co-operative. We would be reluctant to leak to your gutter press the relationships you enjoyed with former cabinet ministers at the Winchester public baths, but if necessary we will do so. Now please let us talk of cricket.'

'I will inform Moscow that you've been absolutely beastly to me,' Sir Evelyn sulked. 'I know it wasn't Mumm's '73, but it was very nicely chilled! Oh all right we'll dredge up what we can. And I suppose I could effect an introduction to Reg Peat, the first-class umpire. He's the only Communist sympathizer I can think of off the top of my head who's got anything to do with the wretched game. He's bent of course – in all the wrong ways. And he's got exceedingly itchy palms!'

'Thank you. I would be pleased to talk with this Empire disloyalist.'

'It will mean a trip to Colchester – a perfectly grisly place!'

'I will leave by first-class train tomorrow morning.'

'By the way,' Sir Evelyn called from his Directory period chaise-longue as Smirnov was about to exit, 'who's paying for this expensive little operation?'

'You are,' Smirnov told him.

'You mean the poor, sodding British taxpayer again!' Sir Evelyn irritably waved him on his way.

3

THE UMPIRING QUESTION

Reg Peat came to the door of his semi in slippers. With an almost toothless smile, he explained that standing played the devil with his feet, and that he was obliged to put them up on every possible occasion that first-class cricket was not being played.

'I don't suppose you've brought a bottle of vodka with you?' he said, as he ushered the Russian spy into a cat-audio-video crowded lounge. 'You don't get to see many hard spirits on a first-class umpire's pay.'

'I have a half bottle,' Smirnov sighed, setting his emergency supply on a Hitachi console. 'However it is authentic Caucasian.'

'I wouldn't mind a carton or two of your Russian fags,' his host said, as he poured himself a wine glass. 'There's no taste to the stuff I have to smoke. For sponsorship reasons if you get my meaning.'

'I do not smoke. I carry only a pipe in order to resemble an Englishman,' Smirnov answered coolly.

'Well at least you've got roubles,' the umpire said, baring both his teeth. 'Or so I am reliably informed by our mutual friend, Sir Evelyn Lilliwhite.'

'That depends on the extent to which you could be able to help me.' Smirnov took a stern swig from the neck of his half-emptied bottle. 'Tell me first about your Imperial responsibilities.'

'I'm not sure I follow you, squire,' Reg Peat leered.

'Are you, like your Imperialist Admiral Nelson, ever to be persuaded to turn a blind eye?'

Reg Peat poured himself another wine glass of vodka and took a slow, painful walk over to his double-glazing which afforded a moist view of a field of semis and a segment of Roman wall.

'I'm a fair man,' he confided, 'a sight fairer than most, but I hate bloody Yorkshire. And I don't mean just Sir Geoffrey; I mean every man, son and tyke of them. That lot would sooner spit at you as offer you so much as a crate of Scotch.'

The first-class umpire turned from the window with a vindictive smile. 'I like to think, sir, that in my small way I've been instrumental in keeping those bastards well and truly anchored around the bottom of the Championship table. Like Glamorgan. That's another county I don't buy, sir. I hate bloody Glamorgan.'

'Please speak more slowly if you will. Do I understand you are suggesting that your Imperialist rulings can influence the fortunes of these County elevens?'

'Good gracious me no,' Peat protested. 'At least not so as anyone would notice. But you know how it is with this game of cricket.'

'I do not,' Smirnov said.

His host lowered a bushy eyelid. 'An umpire can get unsighted in the smoke of those Welsh valleys, just as he can in the sleet and shit of those Yorkshire moors. It can get so murky up there, it's not always easy to see if your tyke is plumb in front or whether the ball might have carried to second slip. Then again the wind can do hard things to a man's hearing, it can be hard to hear if the ball made contact with the bat before carrying to the pads for an lbw. Though you can usually hear when your Pudding or your Taff has snicked the ball for a catch behind. Sometimes you can be the only man on the field to hear that snick. Oh yes we can influence things in our small way.'

Smirnov was grateful to his grinning host for that last sentence. Up until then he had been unpleasantly reminded of an occasion when he had been ordered to produce an instant precis on an intercepted conversation between a Chinese divisional commander and his Mongolian quartermaster – unpleasantly reminded both of the sense of total bewilderment and sheer panic.

'You say you can influence things in your small way in these distant moors and valleys. Is it possible you could influence the same things in a Test Match where there are English players?'

'I was afraid that you'd ask that question.' Peat shook his head. 'Matter of fact Sir Evelyn hinted you might be asking something of this nature. The trouble with Test Matches is you've got television, and television means replays – not to mention Richie Benaud and his beady-eyed mob. You can maybe get a few run outs, pay off a few old scores here and there. But you can't really influence things in a Test Match. There are just too many eyes on the ball. Now if you wanted the Roses Match?'

'I require five Test Matches – all to be overwhelmingly lost by England,' Smirnov said.

Reg Peat sank back into his armchair. A cat squealed under his substantial weight.

'I can't see how as I can help you,' he said. 'There's my integrity to think about.'

'We pay in sterling,' Smirnov told him, 'or in any currency of your choosing.'

Peat stared into a blank 27-inch TV screen.

'I could use a Seychelle Island holiday for two or, better still, three. But, believe me, those cameras don't miss a snick.'

'You speak again of this snick. What please is this about a snick which is so important to your rulings?'

Patiently the first-class umpire again rehearsed his Russian visitor in the basics of his craft. In particular, he stressed, the importance of an audible contact between bat and ball to a convincing 'caught behind' decision – at least when the television cameras were eavesdropping.

Smirnov was silent for a time. Then he said, 'It would perhaps be possible to reproduce this snick – by electronic methods!'

'I'm not sure I follow you, squire,' Peat looked at him a little hazily. He had finished the vodka.

'The sound effect would need to be authentic and it would need to be effectively synchronized with the fling of the bat, ideally by an experienced observer in the closest proximity to the batting green,'

Smirnov looked up at his host on to whose flushed and weathered features a smile of low cunning was gradually creeping. 'Perhaps, after all, you will earn your holiday in the Scilly Islands,' the Russian smiled in his own way.

4
GOODWOOD INTERLUDE

The course was empty of horses. The stand and surrounds which would be as colourful as Kew flower beds later in the season were void of spectators and bookies. Perhaps for this reason there was something even more glorious about Goodwood on this cuckoo-echoing May morning. There was not a human or animal to distract the eye's appreciation of the sweeping contours of the most beautiful racecourse in the world.

James Ball, a point-to-point-like figure in bowler and British warm, was trudging over the grass towards a point on the course which, come July, would represent one of the racing world's most coveted finishing posts.

His mind was intent on a certain meeting in another season in another decade. In his mind's ear the sound of the lone cuckoo was slowly growing into the roar of a fashionable crowd. Danny Boy! Danny Boy! It had looked certain that Charlie Smirke on the Queen's horse, Tyson, was safely home; but suddenly, on the inside, Sir Randolph Montgomery's Londonderry Hare was pressing Smirke into a desperate use of the whip.

'It must be Tyson, no, no it's going to be Danny Boy!' The voice of a young Peter O'Sullevan repeated in his memory, like that constantly re-run film of the last furlong of the Goodwood Cup, July 1959. There it comes in slow-motion. Danny Boy's head goes down, as if preparatory to a final lunge at the post, but now you can see the legs have given way and the whole animal is sinking head first to the ground and a young Lester Pigott is beginning a long slide from the saddle.

'Be so kind as to give us a blow-up of that section of the crowd.' Ball could hear himself speaking across the years from a seat in a smoke-filled projection room. 'No there, there! That man in the trilby. Come in on him, if you please. Larger, larger, I want him larger!' The techniques of enlargement were fairly primitive in those days. The figure in the trilby ballooned into a puzzling mass of black and grey dots. 'Reduce it please, further. Yes leave it there!'

They say you never forget a face. True, but better check with the files. Yes, this man in the passport photograph and this face in the crowd are the same. I. Smirnov, seconded to the staff of the Cultural Attaché at the Soviet Embassy in London. They say your eyes miss nothing. True, at least in those days they didn't. Still it had taken hours of squinting, enlarging and reducing before it was finally confirmed that the smudge at the end of Smirnov's raised shooting stick was smoke.

The public was assured that Danny Boy had suffered a fatal heart attack and I. Smirnov was packed off home by the first Aeroflot plane. Fortunately the holiday season intervened. Troublesome Fleet Street editors departed for the South of France and back-bench Tory MPs left for the grouse moors. A small cloud on the blue face of the glorious summer of 1959. In a matter of weeks the whole sorry business was forgotten. But the mystery had remained to tease at James Ball through the decades. Why? Why? Why?

A Range Rover was approaching him down the course, throwing up clouds of dew from the lush green turf. Was it going to run him over? For a perilous second or two, Bally paused to wonder whether he cared. A lifetime of secrecy and betrayal seemed to have blunted some of his zest for living. It was like cricket in a way. As a younger man he would have minded passionately about yesterday's defeat of Kent at the hands of the Australians by a humiliating innings and twenty-two runs, especially since there were only three weeks to go before the First Test Match at Old Trafford. Now he didn't passionately mind who won the Ashes. How bitter can be the confessions Father Time wrings from us, Bally thought to himself as, at the last moment, he took evasive action.

The Range Rover was braking now, so hard it went into a slewing skid, leaving raw mud tracks on the Earl of March's immaculate grass. A heavily built figure in a peak cap and sheepskin coat got out. It was Hector Bootle.

'James, what the hell are you doing at Goodwood? You ought to be in Colchester.'

'I don't see why.'

'For heaven's sake, I should have thought it stuck out a mile – because Smirnov's in Colchester damn it!'

'So I understand from my own informants,' Bally smiled wearily.

'It's no smiling matter, I can tell you James. The PM is furious. Particularly since it transpires the "Oval" are paying for that grisly little Russian's travel and expenses!'

'Is she surprised?' Bally asked. 'After all the "Oval" *is* run by a Soviet agent.'

'You know she doesn't like to be reminded of that!'

'I suppose it hasn't occurred to anyone that it might be time to unmask Sir Evelyn Lilliwhite?' Bally suggested mildly.

'Are you feeling all right, James? Is Jan playing you up or something? By the way how is Jan?'

'She's on her way to Chesterfield,' Bally replied. 'The Australians are playing Derbyshire next,' he added in an undertone.

'Perhaps we should have left you on the shelf,' Hector Bootle mused. 'A chap would have to be mad or senile to suggest we bring in Lilliwhite! It would be goodbye to the Government, and the Cruise missiles I can tell you. And hello Mr nasty little Neil Kinnock!'

'It was just a thought,' Bally sighed.

'A bloody ridiculous thought! Believe me, from the PM down we're worried sick. And chiefly we're worried about you, James! Let's face it we've got one hell of a conundrum on our hands – I. Smirnov who, for some totally inexplicable reason, is hanging around in County Cricket grounds and consorting with decidedly suspect first-class umpires. And we're looking to you to tell us why! Personally, I think the PM has every right to want to know what on earth you're doing at Goodwood – when there isn't even a meeting – instead of sticking to that slippery bastard Smirnov like glue.'

'The answer is very simple,' Ball said. 'The spy may be in Colchester; but the motive is *here*.'

'I'm sorry you've lost me, James.'

'Exactly where your Range Rover is parked to be precise.'

The senior civil servant continued to look blank.

'Danny Boy, Hector. Surely you remember. The Goodwood Cup, 1959? After all it was our first introduction to friend Smirnov.'

'I know, I know, but that's past history now, James.' Bootle stamped his feet like a horse under starter's orders. 'You won't get my point that the action has moved to Colchester!'

'We always assumed it was the Queen's horse, Tyson, they were aiming for,' Ball soliloquized in the absence of an attentive audience. 'A mad, illogical gesture, particularly considering this was a period of détente. All the same we were satisfied that Tyson was their target. He was the clear leader halfway round the course, a clear target. It was only in the last few seconds that Danny Boy put in his challenge.'

'Cricket, James! Kindly concentrate your mind on cricket. It's the only thread we have in this whole web of intrigue.'

'Yes cricket,' Bally agreed with a faraway twinkle. 'Tell me, Hector, who was the owner of the unfortunate Danny Boy?'

'Does it matter?'

'Sir Randolph Montgomery, Ulster millionaire and sportsman. A former steeplechase and motor racing champion and a safe enough pair of hands behind the stumps to earn him an Oxford cricket blue. Sir Randolph Montgomery had so many interests, it's sometimes forgotten that he served as a Test Selector from 1936 to '39.'

'Is your mind wandering again, James?'

'For too long,' the doyen of spycatchers answered with an odd little smirk. 'You see it's taken me nearly twenty-five years to see that it was the former Test selector Sir Randolph Montgomery they wanted to hurt.'

5

SLOANE MORNING

In a service flat behind Sloane Square, I. Smirnov got out of bed and wrapping a towel around his thickening midrift padded to the door to collect the morning's copy of the *Daily Telegraph*.

'I see there are more atrocities in the Lebanon,' he reported on his return. 'Also that the England selectors have announced the squadron for the One-Day Internationals. But these are not serious Test matches, am I correct?'

The girl in the bed yawned. 'Darling I hope you're not going to talk cricket all day,' she said.

'Why not? There must be an interval between love, even love as passionate as ours. What is wrong if we talk about cricket? It is the English sport, no?'

'Because it's bore-jaw.'

'I'm sorry, I do not understand.'

'Bore-jaw meaning bourgeois, silly.'

'Ah yes. Bourgeois. To us a description of a class enemy, to you a desirable indicator of social status,' Smirnov suggested with an intelligent little grin.

'Rubbish. Bore-jaw people are usually dreadfully Naff. They love the one-day games. Daddy said he's stopped going to Lord's since the football crowds started coming.'

'But your father is the Convenor of the Test and County Cricket Board!' Smirnov protested. He did not add that this was indeed the whole point of their casual liaison. Nor did he explain this was the precise reason why, armed with information grudgingly supplied by Sir Evelyn Lilliwhite's deputy, he had seated himself at the bar of the Antelope public house the previous evening with a bottle of Bollinger and waited for the scarf and the girl to fit the MI5 photograph.

'Oh it's all right to listen to cricket on the wireless (not the box – that's Naff) and I suppose it's all right to ask for the score at a cocktail party, providing you ask for the racing results first. But you definitely don't wear an MCC tie or walk around offering people Rover Tickets. That's madly suburban.' She threw back a mane of chestnut brown hair and looked at him with a shaft of tenderness. 'I can see you've still got a lot to learn about England,' she said.

'But how,' Smirnov persisted, 'can your father, Sir Ambrose, serve as an effective Convenor of the Test and County Cricket Board if he refuses to go to Lord's?'

'Daddy doesn't go to Lloyd's any more either, but he still makes pots of money,' she answered with overwhelming logic.

'I would nevertheless be honoured if at your country seat you could find occasion to introduce me to your father, Sir Ambrose.'

'Like that!' The girl in his bed giggled like a Benendon fifth-former. Smirnov looked down at the towel on his waist, and in the process was forced into a reminder that he badly needed to slim. 'But I will be wearing a new pin-stripe suit. I will look quite acceptable.'

'No one wears suits in the country, silly. Unless they're very old tweeds with dog hairs all over them. Besides Daddy doesn't like to meet my boyfriends – I mean the ones that didn't go to Winchester or Marlborough.'

'I only wish to tell him of my profound admiration. . . .'

'Etonians and Harrovians are absolutely out – with Daddy and *Harpers & Queen*. But then you didn't go anywhere did you, you randy old bear!'

Smirnov drew a deep breath, not merely for physical fitness reasons. He was also excercising his powers of mental self-control. 'As a Russian I wish to tell your father of my profound admiration of your English cricket, particularly of my respect for the high standards of good judgement and fair play achieved by your first-class Empires. I wish to tell your father how much I am looking forward to attending the First Test Match at the Old Trafford and to see there your great English Empire, Reg Peat, standing.'

'Reg Peat! You can't be serious,' the girl shrilled. 'I don't know anything about cricket, but I do happen to know he's the absolute SE23 – meaning the pits.'

She had attractive hair and a good complexion, both nourished, no doubt, by privilege and the thriving English dairy industry. The nose was perhaps a little long, but that was not unusual in bourgeois English girls. Certainly the breasts were as ripe and as firm as a young peasant's and she smelt well, even in the heat of ardour. Nevertheless Smirnov was tempted to strangle her. He resisted the temptation on the grounds of doubtful political expediency. All the same it was obvious she was leading nowhere.

'It was an enchanting evening,' he said coldly as he hunted for a clean shirt. 'Now as you know I have many affairs to attend to concerning my timber export business. You too, I am sure, will have work to do.'

'Sloanes don't go to work,' the girl said, snuggling back into the bed, 'at least not serious work. They only do things like helping out with charities or sorting papers in publishing or the Foreign Office.'

'I have my timber contracts to negotiate.'

'It's only ten o'clock,' the girl said, 'why don't we go to Hurlingham – meaning screw!'

'Plank lengths, widths, grains and forest species, these are the matters that must now concern me,' Smirnov said.

'Oh, well,' she yawned and stretched, 'I suppose I could always go and knock up Vincent.'

'Who please is Vincent?' I. Smirnov asked with lukewarm interest.

'Vincent's my Hooray Henry boyfriend. There's no point in having sex with him at any other time. Hoorays are always hopelessly pissed by opening time.'

'Does Vincent Hooray have employment?'

'No, he's with a merchant bank.'

'Sorting papers perhaps?' Smirnov suggested with a twisted smile.

'Hoorays really don't do anything except get pissed . . . I mean nothing serious. Vincent sometimes helps Daddy.'

'How please?'

'Oh just boring things like advising him on the appointment of racing stewards, rugby and boxing referees and cricket umpires.'

'Cricket Empires!' Smirnov exclaimed with rekindled interest. He gave up the hunt for a clean shirt and climbed back into bed. 'Later,' he said, 'I would be obliged to meet your Hurrah.'

6
AT LORD'S

The ball was fast and well pitched up. Botham went down on one knee and swept it for four. The second ball was faster but fractionally over-pitched. It soared into the Warner Stand for six. Lawson tried a scalp-removing bumper. Botham's Duncan Fearnley flashed. The ball rocketed for another boundary over the wicketkeeper's clutching gloves.

'If only he could reproduce this form more in Test Matches,' Ball's neighbour said. 'There's no challenge in this limited-over stuff.'

Botham completed this over with another six and a left-handed swipe for four.

'Hammond would have taken this attack apart,' the MCC Member on Ball's other side commented as, with a loud burp, he loosened his tie and fastened a Beaujolais can to his mouth.

James Ball was forced into the silent observation that an increasing number of MCC Members were noticeably drunk before the luncheon interval. But still it was Lord's! A May morning! A fresh lick of white paint on the Pavilion rails. The run-stealers flickering to and fro! Oh yes there were still some modest pleasures to be derived from this our life, Ball reflected, even though times had changed a little. The old Tavern had gone. The so-called Tavern Stand had come; the once pleasantly half-populated Mound Stand was packed with howling spectators. There was a difference in the atmosphere, too. Once the scent had been a subtle blend of pork pie, linseed oil and fresh, boyish expectancy. This morning the Pavilion at Lord's smelt like a collision between a vineyard and a brewery. Still the sun was shining and young Randall was taking strike.

The first ball sprung from the bat to a first slip that wasn't there and rapped the Pavilion rails.

'If only he could reproduce this form in Tests,' the Member on Ball's left repeated.

To the next delivery Randall fidgeted into a breathtaking cover drive. Outfielders tumbled. The Mound Stand roared like one gargantuan mouth. Ball noticed that the Member on his right had started to cry.

'Surely it's not quite as bad as that,' he ventured. 'Even Hammond might have been proud of that stroke.'

'Don't mention that name please!' the Beaujolais drinker sobbed, ripping open another can. 'It was thinking of Hammond that made me think of my poor dear old father.'

Tears are unexpected and certainly not encouraged in the Pavilion at Lord's. With an embarrassed pout, Ball turned his attention to the spinning scoreboard.

'Ninety-six not out!' the Member on his right howled.

'No, he's just reached his fifty,' Ball corrected.

'I'm talking about my dear old father. He was cruising towards his century and then . . . Damn, I shouldn't have mentioned the word cruising!' A silken MCC handkerchief was unfurled. 'It was cruising off the Albanian coast last summer that did for the poor old Pater – just three years short of his century!'

'Surely a pretty good age,' Ball murmured.

'A pretty good egg did you say! I'll say so!' The Member was struggling to his feet and appeared to be seeking to free his shirt-sleeves from his MCC cuff links. 'I'll knock any man for six who has the effrontery to say otherwise! My dear old father, for your information sir, was just about the finest brain this game ever had! Damn it, he picked Hutton for the Oval in 1938!'

'Who was your father?' Ball enquired a little tetchily.

'Does the name Montague Endcott-Spurling mean nothing to you!' the Member blubbingly menaced.

With nine out of ten it wouldn't have. But James Ball had a long memory and a retentive mind for minutiae of cricket – M. R. K. Endcott-Spurling, Oxford and Gloucestershire, captain 1919 to 1923. More to the point Endcott-Spurling had served as a Test Selector from 1935 to 1938. Oddly enough approximately the same period the Ulster millionaire horse-owner and cricketer, Sir Randolph Montgomery, had served.

'Last year, off the coast of Albania, you say,' Ball remarked with a hint of interest and sympathy.

'Finest yachtsman in the world too,' the Member bawled before he collapsed into incoherent grief.

Botham was out. The run-hunt had slowed, and James Ball had taken the opportunity to remove himself to a seat on the limited rows parallel with the players' changing rooms.

A dead horse at Goodwood, a dead selector off the Albanian coast – was there any connection? Unlikely and anyway forget it, Bally told himself. Lord's was getting noisier, but it was still a retreat, a green place for forgetting the conspiracies and treasons of day-to-day life. Yes, he thought bitterly, and the humiliations of hearth, home and wife. Forget the world beyond the boundary. Think only that was a nice on-drive of young Randall's if he would just remember to put his feet in the right place.

Almost furtively, James Ball CBE leaned back in his wooden seat and began to unwrap his lunch – a pork pie, a slice of fruit cake, a bar of Cadbury's milk chocolate, sacred links with Hobbs and Sandham and long lost days of innocence. But Ball was to re-learn hard facts of life that morning; if Lord's is a sanctuary, the real world has a Rover ticket for any fixture it chooses. Here, alas, was his assistant, honest, dogged young Buster Tolchard, detached at Hector Bootle's request from Bill Kenyon's British Telecom phone tappers, trampling on the feet of infuriated Members to reach him.

Wistfully James Ball re-packed his lunch.

'I've been trying to reach you everywhere, sir. We've lost contact with the bastard. I. Smirnov has gone to earth!' the perspiring undercover man boomed.

'Do you mind sitting down,' a Member behind him growled.

This was actually impossible. Ball himself had squeezed into the last available space on these coveted rows. Buster Tolchard sat down heavily on his knees.

'We had him right under our noses and then suddenly somewhere around Sloane Square the trail went cold,' he panted. 'It's as if the blighter has vanished clean off the map.'

'Some of us are trying to watch the game!'

'Would you mind removing your hat?'

'But don't worry sir,' Tolchard whispered resonantly. 'We've got men at every gate, in every stand – if that bloody little spy makes a move we'll nab him.'

Two more Members voiced their profound indifference to this information.

'Smirnov won't lift a finger until the First Test.' Ball smiled painfully under Tolchard's shifting weight. 'If I know friend Smirnov, he's definitely a man for the big occasion.'

'We've got chaps selling scorecards, disguised as MCC Members, on the heavy roller.' Buster looked proudly along the packed row of seats to the Visitors' Balcony, 'we've even infiltrated some of our people into the changing room staff . . . My God!' His eyes suddenly bulged. 'That's a bit rich, isn't it!'

James Ball followed Tolchard's affronted gaze. The Tourists were in the field. Only the Twelfth Man and the manager were seated in the balcony; but it wasn't at them that Tolchard was gawping. Cool as brass, although in fact the colours were black and gold, an expensive pair of silk knickers was hanging from the rails of the Visitors' Balcony.

James Ball knew immediately they were expensive. He had bought them himself at Harrods, as a present for Jan the previous Christmas.

The Nursery at Lord's attracts little attention on a match day or, indeed, any day. So apart from a few late ticket holders hurrying abstractedly past this minor sward, there was no one to notice a stocky figure wearing a trilby and a conspicuously new tweed suit. Certainly no one appeared to recognize his companion, although umpire Reg Peat's weathered features would have been familiar to any regular follower of the game. And certainly nobody paused to wonder why this pair was so absorbed in the spectacle of an elderly club cricketer, padded up in the nets, struggling to make contact with the fizzing outwingers of a young member of the Middlesex ground staff – not even the few policemen patrolling this cricketing backwater had stopped to examine the sophisticated electronic equipment which had been planted around the net at the batsman's end.

'Ready, sir?' Umpire Peat called to I. Smirnov as the young Middlesex hopeful began another accelerating run up.

The elderly club cricketer waved his bat, mostly in self defence. *Snick*!

'Have you got that Mr Smirnov? That was your snick all right.'

The Russian pressed a 'Fast Rewind' button. Then switched to 'Play'.

' . . . got that Mr Smirnov! That was your snick all right.' The recorder echoed Peat; but no snick.

'You will be so good as to ask the gentleman to repeat that stroke again,' he ordered with hardly concealed chagrin.

7

LETTER BOMBS

The England Selectors named thirteen players for the First Test Match at Old Trafford. The popular papers exploded with angered astonishment at the omission of Ken Crutchley who had scored three centuries for Surrey in the previous week.

I. Smirnov was more concerned at another omission – this recorded only in *The Times*. For here in the smallest of small print it was noted that Umpires H.D. Bird and J.K. Jeffreys had been appointed to stand.

Smirnov immediately did two things. He carried the naked Sloane from his bed into the corridor and tumbled her still sleeping body into the service lift. After her he threw a random selection of shoes, sweaters, skirts and scarves and pressed the lift button for 'Basement'.

Then he walked rapidly down the stairs and out into the street where he headed for the nearest public call box.

'No,' said Sir Evelyn Lilliwhite in his secret office above Simpson of Piccadilly, 'of course I haven't seen the England team for Old Trafford and I couldn't care a hoot what umpires are standing or why they're standing. As a matter of fact I don't read *The Times* any longer. I find the *Daily Mail* is lots more fun.'

In the public call box Smirnov said, 'I have made the most strenuous informal approaches to Sir Ambrose Darcy in order to obtain the selection of Umpire Reg Peat for the First Test at

Old Trafford. These efforts have not met with the success I had been led to expect. I must now ask you, comrade, to apply the necessary pressures.'

'My dear boy, I hardly know Sir Ambrose.'

'My information is that you were together at Cambridge, at the college of Keys.'

'Were we? Well I hardly remember him. But then I wasn't exactly the toast of the rowing set.'

'Comrade, you will know methods of applying pressure to Sir Ambrose. It is essential that Comrade Peat is elected to stand at Old Trafford.'

'Listen sweetie, I'm not your office boy!' The Director of the Security Services answered waspishly.

'I cannot depend any further on bourgeois prostitutes and their intoxicated Hurrahs,' Smirnov told him firmly. 'I must ask you, Comrade Sir Evelyn, to apply the necessary pressures. Otherwise I will be compelled to telephone your gutter press with important disclosures concerning serious immoralities at the Winchester public school baths.'

'You're a dreary boring little sadist. Tell you what, darling, suppose I was to let you have the names of our agents in Moscow?'

'We already have them' Smirnov sighed. 'Now please Sir Evelyn – the necessary pressures.'

The Secret Service Director put down the receiver with the venom of a non-smoking housewife emptying her husband's ash tray. Then he rang for his Totally Confidential Secretary and dictated the following letter.

PRIVATE & CONFIDENTIAL

Sir Ambrose Darcy, MBE
Newbury Castle
Lambourn
Berks

My very dearest Ambrose,

Spring-cleaning in my Albany flat the other evening I came across some old diaries from our Cambridge days. My manservant, Tony (cheeky little brute!) suggested I threw them out. 'Who's going to be interested in this old rubbish?' I believe his exact words were. It's shocking how little reverence young people these days have for the past. Because anyone with any sense of period would see that these diaries, however *jejeune* their authorship, are in their faltering way a marvellous evocation of a world that has utterly gone and must certainly be of some value to social historians and other collectors.

There's an almost touching clarity to the prose of the young diarist who was, of course, my enviably younger self, and not surprisingly, there's *lots* of you in it! The writing is redolent of tender, tormenting, sensual young love – of the kind that 'dare not speak its name'. I read the eager, juvenile handwriting and, with an almost frightening immediacy, I see two young men in a boat, or rather a punt. And not exactly two orthodox young men either, because you, as you remember, were dressed as a Girton undergraduate, complete with a piquant pair of falsies, to avoid unwelcome comment from your Hearty friends. Sometime someone ought to publish these diaries, if only because they're such a jubilant celebration of the Brideshead era, although of course I'd put my foot down if anyone tried to turn them into a TV series with dreary Jeremy Irons and Anthony Andrews. They're really so middle class – they couldn't possibly convey the extraordinary thing we had between us!

Oddly enough a rather sweet girl from *Country Life* – or is it the *News of the World*? – absolutely agrees with me that I should publish and be damned. What do you think?

Incidentally, darling, I was a little hurt this morning to note that you're not allowing my very dear friend Reg Peat to stand in the First Test Match. I know he's not exactly one of us, but he's an infinitely deserving soul, and just for once, and just for me, I would have thought you could have given Dicky the Bird!

Now that I come to think of it, I suppose it's possible that on reflection I may decide against publication of the diaries, just as I'm sure that, on reconsideration, you will see that it makes complete sense to insist that Reg Peat stands in the First Test. I have to bear in mind that any untoward publicity may not be entirely desirable for the Director of Britain's Security Services, in the same way, Ambrose sweetest, that you'd no doubt be hesitant about seeing your photograph in *Country Life* – or the *News of the World* – in your erstwhile Girton outfit. Personally I think you look gorgeous; but your friends at Lloyd's might take a different view, particularly now that nosey 'Mr Clean' is looking into all your Cayman Island operations.

Give my tenderest regards to Heather and the children whom I gather are quite precocious now, and please don't bother to write, either to me or to my Solicitors. Just a p.c. to say that Reg Peat stands will do.

Your loving friend
Evelyn

8
THE FIRST TEST

Time: 10 a.m. on an early June morning. The place: the Stretford End, Old Trafford, Manchester. The weather: slightly muggy but no immediate threat of rain.

A man is standing here in the constantly improving light. He wears a newish trilby and overcoat and is smoking an unlit pipe. He is a man with an appointment and he has come a long way to keep it – not just in terms of the miles, smoothly devoured by Inter-City Express. Behind the journey lie difficult liaisons, tense public phone calls and bleak moments of despair prior to that brief announcement in *The Times* to the effect that F. R. T. Peat would be replacing an indisposed J. K. Jeffreys as an umpire for the First Test Match at Old Trafford.

The investment in time, nerve and public money has been heavy for I. Smirnov. But patience and perseverance have paid off. The first objective in a bizarre mission is about to be accomplished. Immaculately on time the chosen instrument of destruction is approaching.

He seems at first glance to be leaning a little heavily to one side. This no doubt is due to the sophisticated electronic equipment Umpire Peat is carrying in the left pocket of his white coat. But now he is leaning in the opposite direction.

'This seems to be my lucky day, squire,' Peat squinted a conspiratorial greeting. 'Selected to stand for England for the first time since Headingley '75 and now this windfall from Wales.' He patted the rectangular bulge in the breast pocket of his white coat.

The shape seemed bulkier than the piece of electronic equipment with which he had been issued.

'Bless their nylon little socks if the Mid-Wales Glamorgan Supporters' Club hasn't put the hat around and presented me with a touching testimonial,' Peat confided with a double-toothed smile. 'A whole effing crate of Gilbey's London Dry Gin!'

Smirnov's trained nose twitched. 'You have been taking alcohol.'

'Don't worry, sir. It won't impair my judgement. No fears on that score. If those greasy little Taffy bastards think they can buy Peat, they've got another think coming to them. Frankly squire, a few bottles of gin at wholesale discount prices don't purchase integrity!' He thrust a gnarled finger under the Russian's nose. 'This finger still goes up, whenever I see a Taffy plumb in front, or even if there's maybe a few inches either way in it. And if I hear a loud enough appeal against any greasy Glamorgan batsman with a poncey daffodil in his cap – this finger goes up, straight as a ramrod. There can be no compromise on that score, sir. In my book a Taff is always out, unless there're cameras present. And the same goes for the Yorkshire puddings. I don't buy bribery and corruption, sir. Not from a bunch of Celts as has never had the nous to remember me at Christmas time all these years they've been languishing at the bottom of the table!' A gin bottle glinted in the watery Old Trafford sun. 'Would you care to join me in a small libation, comrade?'

Smirnov took the quarter-full bottle and smashed it on the concourse area tarmac.

'You are drunk, you disgusting peasant!' he hissed. 'You are completely intoxicated.'

The umpire clamped a steadying hand on Smirnov's shoulder. 'Don't worry, squire. A few nips never prevented me from standing if you take my meaning. No problems on that score, if you care to enquire among the ladies of my acquaintance. I don't mind whether it's gin, vodka, champagne or a pint or three of port and bitter – come what may this finger goes up!'

'You were contracted to present yourself properly equipped and sober to umpire the First Test Match at the Old Trafford,' Smirnov groaned. 'You are not sober – you are revoltingly drunk!' He opened the palm of his hand and brought it despairingly across the Englishman's florid face. A couple of Mancunian Test ticket holders paused briefly to wonder why an England umpire was being assaulted by a foreign gentleman.

'Rule 187 of the MCC Rules of cricket!' Peat quoted as he stumbled backwards. '"It shall be deemed unlawful to strike a standing umpire, whether during the course of, or during the preliminaries to, or intervals of, play, prior to a definite result having been obtained. . . ." May I duly remind you, sir, that I am still standing!' Peat threw his arms wide as if to emphasize the point, then tipped forward to take the Russian in a bear hug.

'There's one thing I won't stand, comrade,' he confided in a gin-laced whisper, 'and that's want of trust. Question my probity and you question my stability. I'm serious, squire. Show me a man who doubts my honour and I'll show him two fingers!'

To have come all this way, to have intrigued successfully enough never to be obliged to see service on the Chinese border again, only to have your hopes crushed at the last moment by the weight of a collapsing British Empire – these were roughly I. Smirnov's thoughts as he pondered his options.

'Don't worry, squire.' Umpire Peat winked up at him as if reading his thoughts. 'The trigger device is in proper working order, even if the bowels aren't. No problems on that score, guv'nor. The game's in the bag.'

'You yourself have told me that a convincing operation will require the most precise timing – the most instant sound co-ordination,' Smirnov complained bitterly. 'You are in no situation to undertake these precise timings!'

'Show me a stroke 'n' you'll hear a snick,' Peat slurred.

'You have also assured me you will undertake the intricate mission of the planting of the miniature microphones at the battermen's ends. Has this been done? Are you in a condition even for it to be done?'

'Is all in the bag and is all here. No problem, squire!'

Peat plunged his hand into his left pocket and brought out an electronic control mechanism. With it came a small shower of mini-microphones, delicate pieces of equipment, each no larger than a conventional golf tee. As Peat slumped to the ground in order to pick them up, Smirnov swung his toe cap at the umpire's head. There was a good chance these kicks would kill. On the other hand there was just a chance they could knock the intoxicated referee into sobriety. This was the chance Smirnov had to gamble on.

'The good news,' Brian Johnston announced, 'is that play should begin on time here at Old Trafford this morning. The bad news, at least for England supporters, is that England have lost the toss and have been invited to bat. And that's probably a shrewd decision on Kim Hughes's part. There's still plenty of low-hanging cloud about and – I don't know what you think Freddie – there should be quite a bit of early movement off this very green-looking strip.'

'Aye a decent fast bowler ought to be able to exploit this track. I remember at 'eadingley in 1961 . . . .'

'There's still fifteen minutes to go before we see the first ball bowled in what promises to be a jolly exciting and evenly matched series; but I see that Umpire Peat is already out at the wicket and – this is interesting because we've already had a pitch inspection – he's bending over and prodding the turf at the batsman's end. Which reminds me, someone correct me if I'm wrong, I don't believe Umpire Peat has stood in a Test Match since Headingley in 1975.'

''E's not exactly standing now.'

'Well no, because Umpire Peat has now moved to the other end with that very distinctive walk of his and is repeating the same performance there. What do you think he's looking for Freddie?'

'Clams, perhaps.'

'Well the crowd are enjoying it anyway. He's getting a lot of applause, most of it good natured. Freddie, a brief profile of Umpire Peat – one gathers he's quite a character.'

'Aye.'

On the container lorry-packed approaches to the M1, Hector Bootle remarked, 'Really James, I would have thought you might have been able to afford something a little pushier than an Austin 1100 on your index-linked pension.'

'Jan's taken the Rover. She went up to Manchester early.' James Ball smiled ambiguously into a miasma of thwarted energy fumes.

'Has the whole bloody world got to be brought to a crawl because of your wife's insatiable appetites?' Bootle demanded with an irritable edge. 'You know I'm not a prude, James. Personally I don't care a fig how many colonial cricketers your wife shags, but what does concern me – and I can assure you it's concerning the Prime Minister – is that it's you who ought to be at this damned Test Match not that randy old bat, Mrs Ball, if you'll pardon my language!'

'And here they come,' said Brian Johnston. 'England's opening pair. Chris Tavare is looking very closely at the blade of his bat, as if to say don't jolly well let me down and one can sympathize with his feelings because there's still quite a bit of low-hanging cloud about and – I don't know what you think Freddie – there should be quite a bit of early movement off this wicket.'

'At least we've got the ball-by-ball commentary.' Ball indicated the car radio with a cryptic grin.

'The point is, James, we shouldn't be hanging around Hendon . . . .'

'Finchley,' Ball corrected him.

'I don't care if it's fucking Golders Green!' the senior civil servant exploded. 'We should be at Old Trafford, Manchester, keeping tabs on that evil piece of work I. Smirnov and whatever the hell it is he's up to!'

'We're on the motorway now.' Ball was mildly reassuring.

'And we're still travelling at thirty mph!'

'And Tavare plays no stroke at that one,' commented Brian

Johnston, 'except he must have done, because Umpire Peat's finger is up. Yes Tavare is out! Presumably caught behind. Freddie?'

'Well, you can see Chris isn't happy about it. ''Es looking back at Umpire Peat and shaking 'is 'ead. But the fact remains, Brian, there was an audible snick.'

'"*Los vinos tintos distinctos de Bilbao*",' Hector Bootle read aloud from the back of a fuming pantechnicon, 'can't you overtake it?'

'My foot is flat down,' Bally pointed out. He wondered, is the world getting faster or am I slowing down? It never used to require a Rover to overtake a Spanish wine lorry.

'Now here's Gower taking strike, already on ten but I suspect – wouldn't you Freddie – that he's looking to add to that total. And of course nothing would please England supporters more than to see this wonderful young left-hander start the series off with a ton.'

'Apart from anything else,' growled Hector Bootle, 'I'd like to see Gower bat. He'll have to bat for two days at this rate, James!'

'Gower swings and misses!'

'He hasn't missed, Brian. Umpire Peat has given him out!'

'But that's extraordinary, because I was about to say he missed it by the width of a barn door. Trevor, a comment from you!'

'From here it certainly looked as if Gower failed to make contact by a pretty substantial margin. But the fact remains that Umpire Peat's finger is up, and in support of that decision I'm pretty certain I heard a snick.'

'I thought I heard two snicks,' said Christopher Martin-Jenkins.

'Something damned fishy is going on up there. I told you that blackguard Peat needed surveillance!' Hector Bootle howled. 'You paid absolutely no attention to me, James! You insisted on poking around race courses, looking at old footage of British Movietone News, letting that nymphomaniac wife of yours drive off with the Rover, so that we're stuck behind a bloody stinking, awful Spanish gut-rot truck when . . . .'

'Frankly things couldn't look worse for England,' said Trevor Bailey.

'He's damned right!' echoed Bootle, as resonantly as a Swiss mountain.

'Try and relax,' Ball counselled. 'The action, as they say, may be in Manchester; but we won't find the solution there. You see, Hector, I'm afraid it's not as simple as a case of one corrupted umpire. The conspiracy, if conspiracy it is, has deeper and more devious roots.'

'Lamb shoulders arms and lets that go through to the wicket keeper,' commented Christopher Martin-Jenkins. 'Good Lord,' he added. 'Umpire Peat has given him out.'

'That's a curious decision if I may say so, Christopher. As far as I could hear there was no audible snick, Freddie.'

'Listen, there's a snick now.'

'And the batsman is halfway back to the pavilion, Trevor. There must be something funny about the acoustics to this ground,' Trueman wondered aloud.

'In any case,' Martin-Jenkins summarized, 'there can be no doubt that with half of their recognized batsmen gone, this puts England in an extremely perilous position.'

'Did you hear that?' Hector Bootle hollered. '*England's in danger* and you're sitting there with that self-satisfied grin on your face, talking about devious roots. Here give me that wheel!' The senior civil servant threw his considerable weight across the car and wrenched at the steering wheel. The struggle produced an unexpected spurt from the vintage Austin 1100. It coincided with an overtaking burst by the Bilbaon wine container lorry. An unshaven face mouthing soundless obscenities veered across the windscreen.

'*Inglaterra peligrosa* you slimey little turd!' Bootle barked at him as he yanked the steering wheel down to shave the mammoth vehicle's front bumper. 'Now for God's sake step on it, James!' he gasped.

'There's really no cause for excessive alarm, Hector.' Ball smiled opaquely as they shuddered past the Luton motorway exit with the shape of the Spanish wine truck trembling like an enraged animal in the driving mirror. 'I took the precaution of ensuring there were seats for Harry Grimaldi and his Pitch Rollers.'

'Those clumsy Keystone comedians! I hardly think the Prime Minister is going to be reassured by that information, James,' Bootle said. 'Listen, you senile old pensioner, didn't you hear Christopher Martin-Jenkins? Half England's recognized batsmen have gone.'

'We're getting a number of calls from listeners who are watching television with the sound turned down so that they can enjoy our commentary simultaneously,' said Henry Blofeld. 'And the interesting thing is they're all curious to know what Umpire Peat has got in his left pocket. Is it a new kind of light meter? asks Mrs Eileen Purvis from Reigate. Well we might take a straw poll on this while play has stopped for drinks. Trevor, what do you think Umpire Peat has got in his pocket?'

'I have been watching him quite closely through my binoculars and there's no doubt there's a substantial bulge there.'

'Brian?'

'I've noticed he's got this quite distinctive little mannerism – every time the ball is bowled his hand goes to that pocket. Perhaps he's got a bag of toffees in there.'

'I think I can see a kind of miniature aerial,' commented Christopher Martin-Jenkins.

'Freddie? Yes, well Freddie wouldn't care to say what Umpire Peat has in his pocket.'

'What *has* that ruffian got in his pocket?' Hector Bootle demanded. 'We brought you out of retirement to tell us things like this. It's no secret that some of us are beginning to regret that decision, James.'

'So it's England facing a tremendous uphill task with three wickets down and only thirty-one runs on the board,' Tony Lewis recapitulated. 'Here's Thomson preparing to bowl to Randall. Randall, a tense, nervous figure, obviously conscious of the tremendous responsibility resting on his slim shoulders, relieving the tension there by swinging his bat like a golfer waiting to tee off. And that's interesting because there's a snick. There's Umpire Peat's finger going up! And the extraordinary thing is that Thomson has still to deliver the ball! Trevor?'

'While you've been talking, Tony, I had my glasses on the pavilion, which at old Trafford, of course, is just down there to the left of our commentary box and I've noticed something which I don't think I've ever seen in a Test Match before – two extra umpires coming onto the field of play.'

'My memory goes back a bit longer than yours Trevor, and I must confess I'm stumped too. I can't remember ever seeing more than two umpires standing in a Test Match. What about you Freddie?' Brian Johnston appealed.

'I've never seen a Test Match like this, Brian.'

'Well this is quite unprecedented,' Johnston microphone-hogged, 'because these two white-coated gentlemen are taking up position at Umpire Peat's end. And one of them is going through his pockets.'

'I wonder if anyone else has noticed their boots. I've got my binoculars on them now and they look extraordinarily black and shiny,' Tony Lewis poeticized, 'almost like policemen's boots.'

'Well now at least we've got the answer to what Umpire Peat has got in his left pocket. It looks like one of those radio things you see young people listening to on trains. What do they call them Freddie? Walkabouts? Anyway they're talking earnestly to Umpire Peat out there. What do you think they're saying to him, Trevor? Perhaps they're asking for a piece of music.'

'It certainly hasn't been music to England's ears.'

'Well that's true because the new umpires are playing with the mechanism. And now we're getting the sound we've heard all morning during this disastrous first session for England – snick, snick, snick!'

James Ball leaned back a little further in the driving seat and allowed himself the luxury of a perfectly uncomplicated smile.

'And now all the umpires are going off! At least the two new umpires are going off with Umpire Peat between them. I don't know about you Tony, but I can't remember ever seeing three umpires going off in a Test Match – at least not in perfectly good light.'

James Ball turned to Hector Bootle with the ghost of a wink. 'I told you, Hector, I had taken the precaution of seeing that Harry Grimaldi and Pitch Rollers were on hand.'

No answering wink of gratitude was returned. 'Well they've left it a damn sight too late,' the senior civil servant bellowed. 'There's only Botham left now!'

9

STEPHANIE

A hawk appeared to be hovering in the panting blue skies above Cap d'Antibes. Then slowly it revealed itself to be a bird moving at speed. It arched around the point of the Cap and threw a glancing shadow over Eden Roc. The wings dipped and caught the gold of the sun lounging over the Gulf of Juan. Soon a bird-watcher without binoculars was able to make out a more thrilling outline than a mere bird's, as the hang-glider hovered in to land on the deck of the most opulent motor cruiser in the harbour of Juan Les Pins.

Two white-coated deck hands hurried forward to help from the harness a breathtaking bikini-clad figure. The girl shook out a mane of auburn hair, vivid as a Riviera sunset, and advanced to accept a chilled glass of champagne from a proffered silver tray and the warm applause of a party which included a number of eminent European bankers, US Senators and NATO officers on leave without their wives. Two luscious lips accepted these salutations with the veneer of a smile. Then the girl and her golden body advanced voluptuously towards an exit down a silver-railed companionway.

A prominent member of the US Government waylaid her on the polished cedar steps.

'Stephanie,' he breathed, 'it's OK about that uranium mine in the Andes. I got the deeds here. But, hey honey, the understanding was it's gonna be just you and me from here on in. I don't want to seem censorious, but I couldn't help noticing there's a guy waiting for you in your cabin. Lose him, darling.'

'You're not the only man who gives me presents,' she drawled.

'Stephanie,' he grappled with her, 'you gave me your solemn undertaking.'

She said: 'You will please to take off your hands from me. Otherwise I will ring to have you shown overboard. Yes Walter, from this morning this is my yacht.'

'You're gorgeous, you're adorable, but goddamnit you're ice!' The portly US Secretary staggered backwards. 'How could I be crazy enough to get fixated on an iceberg like you?'

'You know Walter, I must do as I wish to do. I cannot be tamed. Otherwise I am not Stephanie,' she explained as she extracted the deeds from the breast pocket of the American's lightweight yachting blazer and shut her cabin door firmly in his face.

A man in a double-breasted suit was sitting on her downy bed. He also wore a moustache which, like the suit, suggested it had seen better days. The cigarette drooping from his lips was clearly just one of a chain. The already exposed black silken sheets and pillows were here and there grey with ash. In the Côte d'Azure circles he was known as Count Grigor Astonov, a Tsarist Russian title. But Stephanie knew better.

'I am to tell you the English have succeeded in drawing the First Test Match at Manchester,' the visitor said, stubbing out his cigarette in an onyx jewel box.

The girl threw a black towel over her golden shoulders and sauntered over to a silver-fixtured shower unit. 'Am I supposed to be concerned?' she enquired negligently.

The visitor wedged another Marlboro cigarette between his yellow teeth. 'Botham and Taylor put on 187 for the seventh wicket,' he reported, 'thus taking England, after the early disaster, to the respectable total of 293.'

'You're fascinating me,' Stephanie called insincerely from the shower unit.

'On the second day no play was possible on account of the rain,' the Count continued, looking without undue interest at the silhouette of a heart-stopping body, doused with steaming water.

'Why do you trouble me with this information?' the glorious silhouette wanted to know.

'On the third day, Randall came to England's rescue by taking five wickets for 42.'

A steaming Venus emerged from the shower unit. 'That is impossible,' she said. 'Randall is a batsman, not a bowler.'

The counterfeit aristocrat removed his cigarette to give her a crooked smile.

'Good. The Controller merely wished to test your knowledge of cricket. The bowler in question was, of course, Robert Willis.'

'Don't they know I am expert in all sports?' Stephanie called from an extravagant wardrobe of scanty clothing. She added, 'Personally I consider cricket is the most boring.'

'And the games you are playing on this pretentious motorboat are stimulating?' the visitor asked with a yellow-toothed leer.

'They are not demanding, but they are profitable,' her bare shoulders shrugged. 'Sometimes we play *chemin de fer*, and I am always the bank. Sometimes we play at Truth and Consequences and I am always the interrogator. A little later perhaps we will play at circuses and I will be the ringmistress. At sea these gentlemen can become quite bored.'

'The information is satisfactory, but not spectacular, or so I am led to believe.' The visitor tapped a Marlboro tip on a cigarette case from which the silver plate was flaking like mica. 'Control is also under the impression that you are retaining an unreasonable percentage of your . . . er . . . acquisitions for illegitimate expenses.'

The girl turned from the wardrobe and placed her hands on her hips in an exaggerated parody of a model's pose. Apart from the gold band at her throat she was wearing only a white silken scarf knotted between her bosoms and a pair of boy's tennis shorts. 'I would be naked,' she said, 'if I had to dress myself on the expenses they are paying me.'

'In any case,' the visitor exhaled, 'your operations are to be moved to England. Your instructions will be forwarded to you by another courier. In the meantime, comrade, I am permitted to inform you that it is your knowledge of the English cricket more than your more obvious skills which has earned you this promotion.'

'Cricket is a game for old men,' Stephanie answered sulkily.

'You will be playing it to the death,' her visitor grinned.

10

VISITING HOURS, STRANGEWAYS

Reg Peat did not appear to notice the new tone of urgency in Smirnov's voice. Besides he was not to know the reason for it. A ciphered message had reached the Russian agent through Sir Evelyn Lilliwhite's office.

Decoded it had read:

> BBC broadcasts of First Test Match, Manchester, have been monitored. Supreme Control is dissatisfied with the results obtained. An additional agent will accordingly be assigned to the mission. She will be liaising with you; but reporting directly to Control. Details will be forwarded to you by separate courier. In the meantime you are requested to improve your personal performance, using your own contacts.

This was the spur which had pushed I. Smirnov down the dark corridors of Strangeways and now prodded him forward on a hard chair to enquire, 'These stoppages for refreshments – how often are they occurring in a Test Match? Are they occurring at specified intervals? Will there be refreshments notwithstanding the weather and the condition of the play?'

On the wrong side of the grill in the prison visitors' room Umpire Peat indicated that he had urgent matters of his own on his mind. 'Stuff that! You've got to get me out of here!' he bellowed.

'Of course. That will be arranged,' Smirnov placated. 'But first I require to dig your brain concerning these refreshments. Who is it who brings them onto the field? I would have anticipated it to be a servant. However at the Old Trafford this serving man appeared to be dressed as a cricketer.'

'The Twelfth Man brings the drinks on. Now get the bloody machinery in motion, Russkie, I want a free pardon, handsome tax-free compensation and a golden handshake towards an all-paid-for retirement for three in the Seychelles. Because, let's face it, even when you've proved my innocence, I'm never going to be able to stand again in this country!'

'What please is the Twelfth Man?'

'That's another thing that's going to cost you.' Umpire Peat raised an admonishing finger. 'My good name! My repute was my livelihood, as priceless to me as my two poor old legs. You people have taken that from me – and you'll have to pay, as surely as a driver who's had a few has to pay the ballet star whose legs he's run over.' The two teeth glinted in a half-crafty, half-murderous smile. 'You realize I can take you to the cleaners in the law courts!' he rasped.

'This Twelfth Man. He dresses as a cricketer but in reality he is a butler? It is perhaps a device to convince the proletariat that there is equality of opportunity in this elitist game?'

'The Twelfth Man is the bugger who doesn't get picked for the Eleven. Okay?' Peat fumed from a furnace of inner frustrations. 'Now let's start talking turkey!'

'So this Twelfth Man is a cricketer who has not, as you say, "made the Club". Accordingly he is publicly humiliated with the demeaning task of serving soft drinks to his class superiors.'

'Have you tasted the food in here? Have you any idea what it's doing to the poor old bowels?' the ex-umpire appealed loudly.

'Such a man would perhaps be easily bribable,' I. Smirnov mused aloud. 'His social resentment could be exploited to the Party's advantage. He would perhaps consent, for a price, to carry onto the field drinks containing disorientating drugs.'

'Just a minute Ivan!' Peat punched, like a wasp-worried heavyweight at the dividing grill. 'You're not paying out any more roubles till I get satisfaction. I can slap enough injunctions on you lot to break the bloody Kremlin bank. So let's deal with me first, shall we?'

I. Smirnov rose from his seat at the grill like an absent-minded composer in the grip of a leit-motif. 'Yes, yes,' he murmured, 'I will be taking all necessary steps to facilitate your imminent release.'

'Not so fast, sonny!' Peat sought to thrust thick restraining fingers through the mesh that defined the limits of his freedom. 'Frankly I don't look for trouble, but if I'm pushed I can turn very nasty.' A contorted face wrestled for recognition in the miniaturizing framework of a prison grill. 'Don't think I don't have friends! For your information, I've got contacts in the media, the legal profession and the alternative side of the Law. No problems on that score, squire! I could make things very, very hot for you, you little Red bastard! If I had a mind,' his voice grew in volume as Smirnov's back neared the exit of the prison visitors' room, 'I could blow your whole kinky operation! I could get you thirty years in Siberia!' Reg Peat hollered as he was led humanely but firmly back to his cell.

In the public phone box outside the gates of Strangeways Prison, Smirnov put through a call to Sir Evelyn Lilliwhite on his private line.

'I have a further request to make to you,' he said. 'I wish you to use your influence to obtain a death sentence for the Empire Reg Peat.'

'My dear boy, are you feeling well? Have you been dipping a little too freely into your excellent vodka? We haven't hanged anyone in this country for twenty years, not even for mass murder! Much as I would love to see that disgraceful old reprobate swing, I couldn't fix it even if I was *the* Queen!'

'Then you will arrange for him to be liquidated in his cell. This Peat is now a liability to the Party!'

'I'm sorry sweetie, it just isn't on. Well you've seen around the office haven't you? Nothing but debs and a few dear boys without the business sense to earn a living in antiques. Can't your own people do it?'

'I will be obliged to leak to your gutter press certain information if you fail, at the least, to ensure for Empire Peat a prison sentence for life, with no visiting privileges,' Smirnov snapped and hung up on the answering burble of protest. Then he caught a taxi to Ringway Airport and London and Lord's.

11

NETS

Home, or nearly home, from Whitehall and the stridently voiced unease of Hector Bootle and his colleagues. As he had so often done after these ritual ear-bashings from the nervously powerful, James Ball asked the taxi driver to drop him at Lord's, thus permitting himself to walk the last few hundred yards home through the tranquil greenery of the Nursery End.

The England team was at the nets preparing for tomorrow's Test Match. The names were modern – Gatting and Botham, Gower and Lamb – but the figures and the movements they were making seemed comfortingly timeless. Was that young Gatting or was it Lamb? It hardly mattered. The bat he was wielding was conforming to the same arc prescribed by Hammond, Hobbs and even Maclaren, just as those two perspiring young pace men (Foster and Dilley weren't they?) were tracing airy semi-circles on a masterprint established by legendary bowlers like Statham, Larwood and Richardson before them. So many cricketers preparing for so many Test Matches had been crammed into this little green space, an elderly man could be excused from fancying that the young ones were treading on the toes of predecessors still too fluent in movement to be dismissed as ghosts.

Another thought struck James Ball as he paused to watch England at practice, resting on his umbrella like a non-striker at the bowler's end resting on his bat. No, it was too intense to be a thought – it was a stab of apprehension, even fear. How terrible it would be if this great, white-clad wheeling procession was ever to be brought to a halt!

His mind floated back to an August afternoon at the Oval. Hutton bowling his leg-breaks – a rare sight in any Test Match – in an attempt to buy West Indian wickets. Hammond as statuesque as Mozart's Il Commendotore at first slip with the weight of more than captaincy on his shoulders. The gasometers seemingly sagging under the pressure of coming events. All round the ground there is a sense that more than a season is dying, worse than football is coming. And the explanation is not far to seek. A newspaper is blowing across the ground from Hardstaff at square leg to Paynter at deep third man. It crumples like an exhausted fielder against the railings of the Members' Friends Stand. It is an early edition of the *Evening News* and sufficient of the headline is visible to understand its meaning – HITLER . . . POLAND! The Oval, August 1939. He wondered then if he was not a spectator at mankind's final Test.

Another yesteryear afternoon drifted across his mind. Blue skies above Lord's. Blue and khaki uniforms in the pavilion. The RAF against the Army, or was it the Navy? In any case, out of the blue coming the putt-putt sound of a motorcycle with engine trouble. Only as everyone knows by now this is a machine with built-in engine failure. Batsmen, fielders and spectators take a dive. For seconds, seeming like hours, the future of Lord's is at the mercy of the dipping nose of a pilotless bomb. Then with a last gurgle of energy the V1 limps onwards to explode somewhere in Kilburn. Batsmen and fielders pick themselves up. The game goes on.

Ball remembered another season. The encouraging headlines of an almost idyllic series against South Africa wiped away by the news of two missing diplomats – two more time-bombs that were to explode much closer to home than Kilburn. For a while, indeed, it had seemed that Burgess and Maclean and those like Tristan Field who were to scurry after them had swept away all the honour of England. All that was meant by cricket.

Suddenly something very near to irritation creased across Bally's bland countenance. How dare they try to tamper with this game of ours! he exclaimed in the depth of his soul. They had failed in the past. He resolved they would not succeed now.

12

THE TWELFTH MAN

This time I. Smirnov was taking no chances – nothing was going to be left to incompetent subordinates. A forged red and gold MCC Member's pass provided by MI5 was the only form of co-operation he had sought. The rest would depend on his own observations and effort.

The official at the pavilion entrance gave his counterfeit pass only a cursory glance before he waved him into the hallowed portals. He moved quickly up a small flight of linoleum steps and sidestepped into the Long Room, and here a kind of panic overwhelmed him.

He had sat through many official lectures on English bourgeois society. He had come to the conclusion that they had only a slight connection with reality. The streets of London, even the allegedly more fashionable districts, were not strikingly more opulent than those of Moscow. Yes, there were more cars; but apart from the occasional Arab limousine not many signs of spectacular wealth were observable. Nor, apart from the occasional violent traffic warden, was there much evidence of official repression. It seemed that even plutocrats of authentic power like Sir Evelyn Lilliwhite lived in as modestly sized apartments as the proletariat, arguably with more antiquated furniture. In fact up until this moment I. Smirnov had been slipping towards the heresy of believing there was not all that much difference between East and West. Now the difference hit him like an icy blast.

What was it about this room that sent a spreading terror all the way down to his knees? No one was threatening him. Only one ancient man had turned from his binoculars to give him a bleary glance. He decided it must be the total strangeness of this immense room which had obliged him to reach for the support of a steadying wall.

Surrealism is unfamiliar, if not actually forbidden, to Russian eyes and a familiarity with Dali, Magritte and even Tenniel might have helped Smirnov to come to terms with the visual impact of the place. As in *Alice in Wonderland*, which he had neither read nor seen, the world in this corridor of a room seemed to have turned upside down. Old men with spy glasses and binoculars were seated on babies' high chairs while around them tiptoed reverential young men, like parents overawed by their progeny.

Beyond the shaded glass panes he assumed the Second Test Match was taking place, for some of the younger men were straining for a view. He noticed however that if they pushed themselves too far forward they risked a petulant glare from the baby-pensioners in their high chairs.

England is still ruled by the privileged past, and will be for the forseeable future, Smirnov's instinct suddenly signalled to him, since its privileged old aristocrats are nursed as carefully as infants.

And now the Russian agent became aware of all the eyes that were looking at him. Beady ancient eyes staring at him out of gilt frames and the peaks of ludicrously small caps. The infantile past was reinforcing the senile present with its visible contempt for the future.

Most alarming was the full-size portrait of a bearded schoolboy with a midget's cap on his head, principally because the Russian had an eerie feeling he had seen it before. Then he remembered where. This monster with the rolling eyes had been a key slide in Professor Yakov's Moscow lecture.

'W. G. Grass!' he exclaimed with total recall.

'Hsssh!' cautioned an old aristocrat in his high chair.

The younger men turned on him with silent reproach, as if to say 'now you've woken baby!'

Perhaps Professor Yakov was not entirely crazy, Smirnov decided behind his blushes. Perhaps in some way, inexplicable by dialetic, this game is the secret of England's power and this room is its perverse control centre. He experienced a spasm of conviction that his mission had an essential purpose. It was right that this sinister pastime should utterly be destroyed.

'Please,' he whispered to the youngest and least hostile looking member he could accost, 'would you be so generous as to direct me to the English changing rooms?'

'Far door on your right and straight up the stairs,' said the Secretary of the MCC.

No complications about finding the right door. A sign fixed to it read 'ENGLAND DRESSING ROOM. PLEASE KEEP OUT.' Smirnov found the door yielded. As he had calculated, but hardly dared to imagine he would find, a man in an England blazer and flannels was busy pouring a jug of fruit juice into a tray-load of paper cups. Here was the Twelfth Man and the anticipated refreshments. If his calculations were correct, and they had proved remarkably accurate so far, he would shortly be carrying them out into an arena where the England team were fielding – in a matter of twelve minutes, thirty seconds to be precise.

'This is surely a degrading occupation for a State athlete such as you?' I. Smirnov addressed the broad shoulders of Hampshire all-rounder Maurice Romsey. 'Your masters have misled you into believing your fine physique is to be mobilized by your country at the highest competitive level. You have been promised the opportunity to win medals and the grateful acclaims of your co-nationals. You find now you have been betrayed. You are required to carry onto the grass the lemonade like a menial butler.'

'Pardon, but who are you?' Maurice Romsey turned from the tray to enquire. It was certainly true that he was a sportsman of impressive physique.

'A friend,' the Russian spy was quick to assure him. As if to emphasize the point he held up a £20 note. 'Yes I am your friend,' he reiterated, 'it is your captain and his discriminating Selectors who are your enemies.'

'Do you work here?' the Hampshire all-rounder wondered. A shadow of suspicion was passing over his bland, sun-tanned features.

'The Twelfth Man!' Smirnov scathingly exclaimed. 'What a humiliating classification they have awarded you. Is it, perhaps, their envy of your strong proletarian muscles, comrade, that compels them to insult your virility with the name of but a Twelfth Man?'

'I'm not sure you should be here,' the Hampshire seamer and forcing left-hand bat pondered.

'For your sake, comrade, I am here.' Smirnov sketched his weary face into a brave attempt at a disarming smile. 'Together we will play a little joke on your exploiters and you will go home to your good wife or mistress with £20 to spend on luxuries to which she is unused.'

'I think you'd better hop it, or I'll call the Secretary,' Romsey told him with apologetic menace.

Smirnov produced the sachet. Ideally he would have preferred to hold it back until he had had more time to fertilize the seed of subversion which he had planted in this hulking peasant's clearly restricted brain. But time was running short. By his watch there remained only six minutes, forty-five seconds before the drink tray was scheduled to make its appearance in the arena. 'You call this in England, I think, a prophylactic,' he lied. 'It will have the minor effect of causing your eleven men to vomit a little, perhaps to shit in pants. It will be a good joke, yes? But more important, do not interrupt me please, it will ensure that the majority of those selected elitists are incapable of cricketing. Despite the class prejudice of your Selectors it will leave them no alternative but to beg your participation in the national team.'

'Are you thick or something?' Maurice Romsey enquired after a pause for reflection. 'Listen, no one plays silly buggers at Headquarters. I've only played the one time for England – and that was against Sri Lanka. And I mean to be picked again.

Believe me, you don't win an England cap by fooling about with farting powder at Lord's.'

'They will have no other option but to give you this cap,' Smirnov earnestly cut in, 'you are the Twelfth Man, yes? Your eleven superiors will be incapacitated in the latrines.'

'You don't understand – are you foreign by the way? – there are people in this game who would give their right arms to be seen out there in the middle at Lord's, even if it's only to carry on the drinks. You get noticed. You get remembered out there. You get your face in front of the TV cameras. You get your card marked by the people who matter. That's important in this game. There are other perks, too,' Romsey revealed. 'This afternoon I'm due to be presented to Royalty with the rest of the lads. Now if you'll excuse me . . . ' The burly Hampshire man was turning back towards his tray of innocuous drinks. In a few seconds he would have the tray in his brawny hands. Very soon there would no longer be time to refill those cups should the servile giant be obliged to let them fall.

'England – the most lousy team in the world!' the Russian spat out with deliberate provocation.

'What did you say?' The Twelfth Man's bowed head came up from the drinks table.

'England – bloody useless!' Smirnov sorrowfully taunted, because a crucial part of the plan had depended on the working man's innate sense of the injustice of things.

Romsey advanced towards him without his drinks tray, although both his fists were raised. Smirnov gave him a hard kick in the abdomen which doubled him up and brought his solid neck nicely within reach of a concussion-causing hand chop. With eyes filled with pity for himself, Smirnov watched the Hampshireman crumple to the floor. You have made my assignment so much harder for me, he thought.

He stepped over the senseless body and raced to the table and the soft drinks tray, tearing open the sachet in the process. As evenly as time still allowed, he distributed a KGB special (codeworded SIBERIA), a formidable cocktail of paralysis and halucination-inducing drugs blended with a variety of chemical agents, one of which had the property of simulating the extreme effects of rabies.

Now panting both with nervousness and expended energy, I. Smirnov stripped down to his underwear and stowed his suit in a locker marked MR I. T. BOTHAM. The Twelfth Man's white flannels came away quite easily. The problem was to remove his white shirt and blazer. Another toe cap thrust in the abdomen did the trick. The Twelfth Man recovered sufficient consciousness to raise his torso from the dressing room floor for a few precious seconds. In this drastically limited time, I. Smirnov was able to relieve him of his shirt and his England blazer. Another spurt of adrenalin saw to it that the half-naked body of the Hampshireman was bundled into a locker marked MR R. G. D. WILLIS.

With only seventy-five seconds to spare, I. Smirnov was in a position to move towards the dressing room door, tray in hand, in the fairly convincing disguise of England's Twelfth Man. True he lacked the height, the physique and the sun-tan of the official discard; but the Russian agent was banking on the fact that cricket was an essentially selfish game. There was just a chance that these over-indulged Test champions would be too self-preoccupied to bother about the identity of the England underling who was serving them with soft drinks.

He was just about to open the door with a patent leather shoe – his hands being fully occupied with the drinks tray – when he found it was opening for him.

An expensively scented woman, dressed as it were for Ascot, was sidling in. Her cheeks and chin betrayed her as a woman of a certain age; but her mascara-framed eyes had an intensity that defied time, and her lips were as red as strawberries.

'You're the new boy, aren't you?' Jan Ball breathed. 'Welcome to the Club.'

She slowed her headlong advance to subject the Russian to a brief inspection – big, brown passionate eyes in conflict with the blinkers of short sight. 'You seem a little startled to see me,' she decided. 'No doubt you were under the impression that ladies are not admitted to the pavilion at Lord's. Maurice – it *is*

Maurice, isn't it? – I'm no lady!'

'Excuse please, it is the hour for refreshment. I am destined with this tray in the arena.'

'It's awfully hot weather, isn't it, darling? I could do with a long, cool drink myself.' She reached for a lethal lemon cocktail. The attempt brought them into physical contact.

'What a strong, confident hand!' Mrs Ball observed as her thin, braceleted wrist wrestled in Smirnov's anxious grip, anxious because in order to restrain her from drinking he was obliged to balance the tray on the palm of his right hand. 'Of course you're a left-hander, aren't you? A very forcing left-hand bat; but oddly enough a right-hand bowler. I like that in my cricketers.' An enormous pair of eyelashes fluttered at him. 'I like ambidexterous all-rounders!'

'Please let me pass. Otherwise I will be reprimanded by the Selectors.'

'Oh don't worry about the Selectors, darling.' Her free hand moved with a jangle of silverware to stroke the three embroidered lions on his England blazer, 'I know them all intimately. And they're all little boys at heart. Just tell them you've been having a drink with Jan – they'll understand what you mean.'

'Duty to England,' Smirnov found himself murmuring. Then protesting. The woman's free hand had dived to his trousers.

'I love clean white flannel,' she exulted. 'I suppose it was not being allowed to play cricket at school, a kind of Freudian hang-up you know – they said lacrosse was better for deportment. I've been a cricket groupie ever since I left school. And that's going back a little while.'

Smirnov now made an attempt to sidestep her, releasing her would-be drinking hand in order to permit himself a wider arc. Two powdered arms wrapped themselves round his waist. 'Of course I adore the stars,' she confided, 'but I dig the up-and-coming players too. I love the freshness of a new England blazer – you've only played once for England, haven't you, darling? Just the once against Sri Lanka. There's something about an England blazer with all its future in front of it that – I don't know – "turns me on" as they say. Oh yes Maurice, I believe we'll go a long way together for England.' She brought her face close to his and whispered huskily in his ear. 'I've got the feeling you're chock full of runs.'

At this range Jan Ball's expensive scent was overpowering, like the door of a perfume factory thrown open on a suffocatingly hot afternoon in the South of France. The Russian used his elbow to make a vicious thrust for freedom. His assailant fell to her knees: but she was not to be counted out. In fact she was now embracing him around his knees with the tenacity of a rugby full back.

'Don't try and fight it, darling,' she urged. 'Never be afraid to play your natural game. Believe me,' she reached up to tug at his borrowed shirt, 'your career won't suffer by having a little drink, as they say, with Jan. On the contrary you've only got to look in Wisden to see what Jan can do for a novice.'

She was right in a way. He shouldn't have tried to fight it. The effort of freeing his knees brought her arms sliding down to his ankles in an ever tightening hold. Now he only had to make an attempt at movement to overbalance. He made the attempt and sprawled forward on his face. Ahead of him the drinks tray crashed into the dressing room door. A cloud of steam rose hissing from the room's bare floorboards as the fruit drinks and their chemical additives inevitably spilled.

'You're quite a pudge pot, aren't you?' Jan Ball playfully fondled while her horse-thin legs took the Russian's buttocks in an embrace of black silk hose. 'That's the beer I suppose. I know you Hampshiremen, you're terrible beer topers, almost as bad as Somerset and Gloucestershire. And my adorable Aussies. But then of course they drink lager which isn't so fattening and is much better for their sex lives. Believe me I know. Oh, I'm quite aware there are wagging tongues who say I've got a thing about all the colonials. But it's really not true, Maurice. I love England nearly as much – the professionals and the amateurs. Though if I have to be absolutely frank, darling, I don't dig the big fella. He will look at me with those terrifying blank eyes, as if I was a West Indies opener or a rival for the

England captaincy. To be perfectly honest I don't think he approves of me. I don't like to feel rejected like that, Maurice. It frightens me.' Without any advance warning she started to scream.

But then there had been no advance warning from the locker. The door marked MR R. G. D. WILLIS had suddenly swung open. The dazed hulk of the England Twelfth Man, naked except for string vest and pants, was unexpectedly lumbering out.

It took Maurice Romsey a little time to adjust to the scene. But once a rough impression had been formed it was instantly rushed to his recently outraged memory.

'*Assault! Murder! Rape!*' he bellowed, loudly enough to wake the Long Room's drowsiest member.

'I told you he hates me, the surly spoil-sport!' Jan Ball confided quivering.

'Do you know if there is another exit?' I. Smirnov enquired with some urgency.

She indicated there was a way. She hinted she had used it once or twice before. Taking his hand she led Smirnov to the laundry chute and, after adjusting her dress, dived in after him.

13
AN ULTIMATUM

'I don't know how you can sit there sipping gin when the Prime Minister wants an explanation on her desk at 9.15 a.m. as to just how an England Test player came to be assaulted in the team dressing room,' Hector Bootle complained.

James Ball reached a weary hand towards the Booth's and recharged his glass. 'He *was* the Twelfth Man, Hector,' he sighed. 'I doubt if Romsey will ever be a permanent fixture in the Eleven.'

'That's hardly the point. The fact is he was wearing an England blazer – and he was robbed of it in broad daylight. In the Pavilion of all confounded places! By the way,' he added, cocking an ear to the ceiling, 'what the hell's going on up there?'

'Jan is entertaining.' Ball smiled like a Blitz survivor, dug out of the rubble with only mildly severe wounds. 'It's a kind of tradition on the Saturday evening of the Lord's Test.'

'Perhaps if you were to get a grip on your private life you might be able to get some kind of grip on this case,' Bootle suggested harshly. 'Let's be honest, James, grip is what's needed in this bloody business, and it's no secret that Whitehall is saying you've lost yours!'

'A first innings lead of 45 can hardly be called a disaster for England,' Ball gently remonstrated. 'If we *can* discern the hand of friend Smirnov in this morning's dressing room "mugging", we can also be pretty confident that he's far from satisfied with his efforts. Apart from the ten-minute delay when they were looking for a reserve Twelfth Man to bring on the drinks, they had absolutely no influence on the course of play.'

'I've just had a report from our backroom boffins. Those drinks had been tampered with, James!'

'They were also spilled,' the veteran spycatcher pointed out.

From upstairs came the sound of movement, as if heavy furniture was being slung about the room.

'If you don't mind me saying so, your wife is a damned noisy entertainer,' Hector Bootle observed. 'But the point I'm making is that you bloody nearly let that noxious little weevil get clean away with it – if those drinks had reached our fellows God knows what the Prime Minister would have said. As it is we have to see her at crack of dawn on a Sunday morning – never her most charitable hour at the best of times – and explain why you haven't put Smirnov in the bag. Why the hell haven't you, I'd like to know? What on earth was that?'

Bootle was referring to a male scream emitting from the upstairs room.

'*A spycatcher*!' I. Smirnov had leapt from Jan Ball's bed and clutching arms to exclaim. 'You are telling me your husband is a *spycatcher*!'

'Come back here darling,' the lady pleaded from a tousled marriage bed. 'Bally may be a tough old counter-espionage agent; but he's a very tolerant husband. He won't mind about us, so long as we don't force it under his nose.'

'Very well, friend Smirnov has slipped the net again; but in any case isn't there an argument for playing him a little longer?' James Ball was arguing. 'You see Hector, I'm pretty certain there's a bigger fish behind him, a very big fish indeed. If you like we can compare friend Smirnov to that unpleasant little species known as a "pilot fish". We need to see which way he's swimming because following him, I have a feeling, is a fair-sized shark.'

'Holy ikons, he is talking about me!' Smirnov gasped to himself as he lay with his ear to the half-open door of Jan Ball's boudoir.

'What are you doing now, Maurice?' she blinked myopically

from her lavender-scented pillows. 'I can't see what Bally's occupation has got to do with you. You're a Twelfth Man, not a Third Man, aren't you?'

Hector Bootle poured himself a hefty slug of Booth's and added a light topping of tonic.

'James, what I have to tell you isn't easy,' he announced, once he was suitably fortified. 'The fact is we're putting a time-bomb under you. Let me put it brutally frankly. You've got until the Third Test to bring Smirnov in. Otherwise there'll be nothing I can do to prevent you being blown right back onto the shelf. I'm afraid your hopes of knighthood will go up in smoke too, James. I'm sorry; but there it is.'

Ball smiled sheepishly. 'I only wanted it for Jan. She would like people to call her a lady after all these years. Still I can take a hint Hector – it's friend Smirnov or my head on a platter. You and your Prime Minister certainly want your pound of flesh, don't you?'

So the husband of this demented old woman is the notorious James Ball, I. Smirnov thought to himself as he crouched in outsized white flannels at the boudoir door. He had heard enough of their conversation to understand that he was its subject. It will be necessary, he decided, for this James Ball to die.

'I don't know why you're kneeling by that door,' Jan called to him. 'You'll find it's much cosier in here.'

14
PRESS CUTTINGS

ENGLAND STUMBLE TO DISMAL DRAW!
The Ron Raphael Report.

Shed a tear for England's captain Bob Willis. He thought he had the Lord's Test in the bag. But the hole torn in England's fragile batting line-up on Monday afternoon effectively punctured those high hopes.

This morning there was just a chance that England's pace attack might pull the necessary rabbits out of the hat. But persistent short-pitching and blatant neglect of length and line saw to it that even the Aussie rabbits were able to play Dilley, Cowans and Foster and Co with the ease of a Viv Richards. It was enough to make Middlesex's Phil Edmonds, passed over again thanks to the Selectors' blind faith in crude pace, wring his spinning fingers in despair. At one shameful moment this evening it looked as if England was going to be battered to defeat. But a last-minute do-or-die effort by skipper Willis just managed to staunch the run-flow. So a sorry England slunk back into the pavilion with a dismal draw as the reward for their earlier match-winning efforts.

After the game a weary Willis said, 'Our bowlers lacked penetration when it counted.' You can say that again, Bob! Meanwhile I can't see much sleep in store for England's Selectors tonight – they're lying awake counting sheep, sheep wearing England sweaters!

'IT WAS JUST ONE OF THOSE DAYS!'
David Gower talking to Len Burrows.

Every Test team has 'one of those days'. It's just unfortunate ours turned up yesterday when with better luck we could have pulled off a thrilling win. No, it wasn't a day 'Both' is going to want to remember and I'm still kicking myself for that uppish cover drive in our second innings, particularly since I had been stroking them nicely until Alan Border took that amazing diving catch. We're offering no excuses; but I'm prepared to take issue with those pundits who insist that 'Dill', 'Cow' and Bob had a responsive pitch to exploit. Believe me, from out at the middle it was obvious that the strip was slowing up with every frustrating hour that passed. The lads learned a lot of hard lessons at Lord's yesterday. You can be sure they won't be lost on our opponents at Headingley!

15
GLYNDEBOURNE SELECTION

With the black bow-tie already in place (the dinner jacket was folded neatly beside the hampers in the boot), the Chairman of Selectors, L. M. S. Partridge, was driving through the lush Kent countryside towards an evening of spiritual refreshment at Glyndebourne.

His wife and sister-in-law were his companions in the speeding BMW and the car radio was switched to Wimbledon. L. M. S. Partridge thanked the blue Kentish heavens it wasn't cricket. He had, frankly, had a bellyfull of the game over the past week. And the newspapers weren't letting him forget it. The way the sports pages were ranting you might have thought he was criminal for having gone into the Test with an all-pace attack on a wicket which had perversely turned out to be favourable to spin. If the truth were to be told, L. M. S. Partridge never wanted to read or hear the word cricket again, notwithstanding the fact that he happened to be Chairman of the Test Selectors.

It wasn't as if there was any money in it, Partridge mentally reminded the skimming elms on the Tunbridge Wells-Uckfield road. He made his money, of course, with Lazard Brothers. Sometimes he even lost a little. But Lazard Brothers never howled at him the way the Fleet Street hacks would howl at him for losing or even drawing a Test. If it hadn't been for his initials he would have been seriously tempted to chuck the whole thing in.

In the deepest recesses of his heart, Partridge knew that to a large extent he had owed his Oxford blue and occasional England cap to those three letters – L. M. S. He was, in other words, the last of a generation for whom a string of initials was a prerequisite for honours on the field. In his case they had had to count for more than his batting average. Again, if he was honest with himself, L. M. S. Partridge would have had to admit that he owed his present Chairmanship to those three magic letters. For England had nearly always had as its Chairman of Selectors an Oxbridge man with a minimum of three initials to his name. Apart from the interregnum of Alec Bedser, it was a tradition that stretched back from his immediate predecessor P. B. H. May to R. W. V. Robins and G. O. B. Allen before him. L. M. S. Partridge was the heir to a dynasty that originated in the mists of time with the half-legendary H. D. G. Leveson Gower. A man did not abdicate from a heritage like this.

'We're going to miss the first act,' Mrs Partridge said.

'There's always a spot of traffic in Uckfield, but we've got a good hour in hand,' answered L. M. S.

'We'll need time to go to the powder room,' his sister-in-law pointed out.

'We don't want to rush in a mad scramble as we did last year,' his wife insisted. 'We must have time to find a nice hideaway for the hampers in the gardens.'

Uckfield had more than a spot of traffic this afternoon. It had a tailback of lorries and coaches, many of continental origin, stalled by a deep defensive system of lollipop ladies exploiting every street corner for mass crossings by school-children.

'Bugger!' L. M. S. Partridge exclaimed, for the reflected sun was visibly sinking on the bonnet of the BMW.

'There's no need to swear,' Mrs Partridge said. 'If you hadn't tried to squeeze in that silly Committee Meeting, we could be relaxing over iced tea and chocolate cake at Glyndebourne now.'

BMW technology finally went some way to make up for lost

time. With ten minutes to spare the Partridge party swept into Glyndebourne's grassy car park. Only the grazing sheep on the overlooking turquoise hillside seemed unaware of the pressure that Time was now imposing on the hurrying opera-goers.

Mrs Partridge and her sister clawed their way out of the BMW and scrambled off in the direction of the pink-walled garden clutching black silk and lamé evening gown hems around their hips. Like a speeding sowing machine, their high heels left two neat rows of punctures in the grass.

'Take the hampers and the seats to the garden!' Mrs Partridge called over her shoulder as she ran. 'I'll leave your ticket with the man at the door!'

L. M. S. Partridge took a deck chair under one arm and lifted the first hamper from the boot. The sheer weight of the thing forced him into the conclusion that his wife came to Glyndebourne for eating as much as Mozart.

Tennis is a customary part of the scenery at Glyndebourne. There are a number of vine-garlanded courts where members of the orchestra and cast can be seen at play between performances. Cricket at Glyndebourne is an altogether rarer phenomenon. In fact, L. M. S. Partridge, setting down his load of three deck chairs and two crammed hampers, felt bound to ask himself if he had ever seen a woman playing cricket at Glyndebourne in his life before.

A net had been set up against the wall of the rose garden and a strip of matting laid across the high-heel-punctured grass. The bowler, an Italianate-looking young man, perhaps a member of the chorus, was pitching consistently short; but it was the striking-looking batswoman who trapped his gaze. The girl was cooly demonstrating that she possessed every stroke in the book – a sumptuous off-drive, an exquisite square cut, a hook of superbly calculated arrogance, a sweetly timed leg glide. All this might not have been sufficient to cause the Chairman of Selectors to forget there were now only four minutes to curtain up. But the girl also happened to be at least as beautiful as her strokes.

'Would you like to bowl to me?' she called in a very slightly foreign accent. 'I need practice against bowling of good length.'

The bell for the first act was ringing insistently enough to silence the summer evening's twittering birds. But L. M. S. Partridge answered the honeyed voice like a Ulysses unbound. He stripped off his dinner jacket, laid it neatly folded on the hampers, and took the ball from the Italianate bowler who immediately vanished, as if on cue.

At Oxford, L. M. S. Partridge had been a useful enough leg-spinner to have accounted in practice games for both M. C. Cowdrey and M. J. K. Smith and once to have rescued the University from a brutal hammering by the Australian batsman Norman O'Neil.

But these were now distant memories and the demands of Lazard Brothers and selecting for England had left precious few opportunities for bowling practice. In the circumstances, he was gratified to see that his first ball had dropped with copy- book precision on the leg stump and was now breaking sharply to take the off-stump's bail. A bronzed leg flashed. A willow waved and the ball was majestically deflected into the back of the net as the girl completed a beautifully executed late cut.

Try her with the googly. Again the length was perfect. This time the ostensible target was the off-stump; but the ball carried sufficient deceptive spin to take the leg stump comfortably. The girl was already committed to a fatal forward prod; but an instinct suddenly alerted her to the true nature of the delivery. In a split second she was on the back foot watching the ball onto the middle of the bat. Then with a flick of her wrists it was fizzing away for a certain leg-side four, assuming there had been no net.

The next ball was a fraction short. She danced down the matting wicket and sent it racing over his head to dent the roof of a Jaguar far back in the car park.

His next delivery was frankly a little wayward both in length and line. But the chase to the Jaguar had left L. M. S.

Partridge short of breath. You might have said he was already hooked before she effortlessly swung the ball over her shoulder to disappear beyond the garden wall to a distant tinkle of shattering champagne glasses.

The girl shouldered her bat and advanced down the matting wicket. As she neared him she took off her white cricket cap and shook free a mane of spectacular auburn hair. Now L. M. S. Partridge noticed that apart from a gold band at her throat she was wearing only a white silken scarf knotted between her magnificent breasts and a pair of boy's cricket shorts unnecessarily supported by his old school tie. He noticed further that she had been playing his bowling in bare feet.

'Tell me,' the girl called Stephanie demanded with a half-insolent smile, 'am I selected?'

She had led him to a grotto which hid them entirely from view. Their feast of food and love had no interruptions, except the distant murmurings of Mozart.

Felici rendecti; amate con moi . . . .

Faraway snatches of benign song had drifted through the scented foliage and the girl had lifted her hand to his cheek and whispered in his ear 'Am I not even more diverting than *Cosi Fan Tutte*?'

But now the music had stopped and they were aware of the hubbub of English voices and a popping of champagne corks. It was, of course, the interval, and soon Partridge was made conscious of a more strident sound.

'L. M. S., L. M. S.! Where are you L. M. S.?' he could hear his wife calling.

'Where have you hidden the hampers?' he could hear his sister-in-law howl.

He started to scramble to his feet in a spasm of guilt and agitation. 'My wife and sister-in-law,' he stammered, 'I must go and see if they're all right.' The girl swallowed another strawberry then turned to close his mouth with a vermilion kiss.

'Do not look so English and uncomfortable,' her velvet voice caressed his ear, 'we are talking about the new England Test team. That is so much more important than your wife and sister-in-law.'

The bells for the second act had long since stopped ringing. So had the increasingly distraught calling of the wife and sister-in-law. 'Where have you hidden the hampers, you bastard?' had been their final vengeful reprise. Partridge and the girl were now alone with burgeoning nature on an enchanted evening.

'You are a sweet man,' Partridge's midsummer night's dream whispered at the crepuscular sky from her pillow on the Chairman of Selector's strawberry-stained shirt front, 'but, you know, you are too loyal to Christopher Tavare of Kent. He has good concentration, a good temperament; yet he will not move his feet to the balls. That is a serious failure in an opening bat.'

'You may be right there, my angel,' L. M. S. Partridge ardently stroked his wood nymph's sunset-tinted hair. 'Suppose we open with Gower?'

'Everything is wrong with selecting David,' she answered dreamily. 'Oh yes, he is a very charming young man, and quite stylish. But you know, he is so vulnerable outside the off-stumps. No seriously, you should study his dismissals. You should see how often he is taken in the slips for flashing at the short-pitched delivery. Will you pass me please some more caviare. I am even after the lobster and the strawberries still ravenous.'

'Perhaps we should hold him back at number Four – let Alan Lamb see the shine off the ball at number Three.'

'That Lamb for the slaughter!' she gently mocked. 'You cannot be serious. Alan is a good South African; but they would not pick him for South Africa and do you know why? Because he cannot play the outswinger. He will dangle at it with his bat, like an animal mesmerized. Please pour me some more champagne and do not think any more about that poor Alan.'

'Randall will certainly have to keep his place,' Partridge asserted when he had broached the last bottle of Veuve Cliquot.

'Darling, that Derek is so fidgety that he is making all of your batsmen nervous. Perhaps he will score a century here and there, but he is always talking to himself, always making the other Englanders feel ill at ease. That is not good for a strong team. You must dismiss Randall,' she emphasized with a massaging hand on his studiously weight-watched stomach.

'I suppose you're going to say I should sack Botham next,' Partridge laughed and heard a falsetto giggle. He realized he was drunk – drunk with love and champagne. He decided he had never been happier in his mildly distinguished life.

'Yes, I am saying that you must not select ever again this Ian. He, too, is making the other England batsmen nervous; because they have not his muscles and they are trying, foolishly, to copy him and getting out. So for all the runs this 'Both' makes, you must think of all the runs that are not being made by his England team-mates, because he is so macho and virile – they feel in comparison like helpless little boys.'

'I never thought of that,' L. M. S. Partridge admitted. 'But then I never met anyone with a cricket brain like yours.'

'You must not flatter me,' she caressed with words and exploring hands, 'you must only believe I have a woman's instinct about these things. Now this instinct is telling me it is time for you to be making very revolutionary changes.'

'Surely we've got to keep Taylor behind the stumps.'

'His hairs are grey, greyer even than yours my poor worried Mr Partridge. Listen to your good counsellor, you must be bold and strong, as you have been strong with me. You must vote for the young bloods.'

'Dearest, divinest angel, you can't really accuse me of not giving youth a chance. What about Cowans? And Cook? And Foster?'

'These are tired, ageing mens,' she insisted. 'They do not any more have the fire in their stomachs. No, you must be daring, you must not care what people are saying – you must appoint very talented, very young mens, like Ken Noads of Essex.'

'I've never heard of Ken Noads of Essex,' the Chairman of Selectors confessed.

Two apricot coloured arms, gleaming like gold in the fading light, reached up to encircle Partridge's neck and pull him down to a pair of strawberry-moist lips. 'My dear friend, you have so much to learn about cricket,' Stephanie purred.

16

CLUBLAND CORONARY

Sir Matthew Glossop had arrived at Victoria Station late on Sunday night from Rapallo. At every stop along the route, scheduled or unofficial, he had leaned from his couchette window to bark at inspectors, porters and linesmen for news from England. Not until the Gare du Nord had a SNCF official obliged with the information that Mrs Thatcher was lunching at Chequers with the Irish Prime Minister. His face was sprayed with infuriated saliva. It was the composition of England's team for the Third Test Match at Headingley that Sir Matthew wanted to know.

The Sealink crossing had been another severe disappointment. A boatload of drunken Englishmen and their queasy womenfolk singing 'Viva Espana' without a thought for the twelve names for Headingley had stretched his patience to breaking point. Only the prompt intervention of a Sealink steward had saved Sir Matthew from being knocked unconscious by a flurry of loaded Duty Free shopping bags.

Alighting from his train at bleak, friendless Sunday-night Victoria, Sir Matthew had only been able to summon the strength to smash his walking stick on the bonnet of a taxi and murmur his Cadogan Square address. He had been too sick at heart and short of breath to enquire of the driver whether he had heard the one o'clock news.

This morning he had awoken to another blow. He had cancelled his order of *The Times* until further notice, as the paperless doormat now bleakly reminded him.

Following England's fortunes over many years had not been beneficial to Sir Matthew's health. He had shaved and dressed as rapidly as his labouring heart would allow. Then he had ambushed another taxi and driven straight to his club.

For over twenty-four hours, Sir Matthew had been in a state of anxiety and stress calculated to undermine the restorative effects of the Rapallo holiday. Now his heart lost another vital beat and his blood pressure took another dangerous leap from the effort of parting a junior member from the Club's one copy of the morning's *Times*.

Sir Matthew thumbed at once to the sports pages, although as it happened the information he was seeking had made the front page. ENGLAND MAKE A CLEAN SWEEP FOR HEADINGLEY, *The Times* cricket correspondent reported with the fashionable sub-editorial jauntiness dictated by the paper's Australian owner.

Sir Matthew skimmed through the report towards the long-awaited names. '"Time for very revolutionary change," declared the Chairman of Selectors this morning. . . . "The moment has come to replace grey hairs with the red blood of youth," Mr L. M. S. Partridge insisted. In your correspondent's view there can be no doubt England is taking a very serious gamble, particularly if the Headingley wicket lives up to its reputation.'

Now Sir Matthew's eyes finally reached the twelve named players. At the second reading they had bulged to twice their normal size. Obscene oaths and then terrifying gasps began to issue from the old cricket enthusiast. Halfway through the third reading Sir Matthew Glossop was seen to pluck at his throat and then to make a failing effort to unloosen his MCC tie. Then he slumped to the club's camel-coloured carpet, as he had never done before noon. A fellow member called Commander Ian Watson RN (Retd), a former Naval surgeon, said that it would be serving no point to send for a doctor.

This was the England team that Sir Matthew's dying hand let fall.

Elvis Brown, Hants (capt)
Ken Noads, Essex
Lionel Pew, Surrey
Benny Blisset, Northants
Simon Bird, Middlesex
Wally Ficket, Derbyshire (wkt)
Nigel Nolan, Lancs
Larry Duck, Warwicks
Gino Carstairs, Sussex
Miles Watford, Somerset
Abraham Udu, Glamorgan
Neil Gnome, Gloucs

The paper landed near James Ball's feet. He did not lean forward in his armchair to pick it up. He was already only too well aware of its contents.

The team announced for Headingley had finally proved to Ball that 'they' meant business. He had sensed immediately he heard the team read out by a stuttering BBC announcer that this collection of nonentities and unknowns was not the work of a third-rate saboteur like I. Smirnov. The team bore the imprint of the Enemy at his most professional and deadly. Hitherto it had seemed to Ball that 'they' had only been playing at disruption, perhaps to satisfy the perverse sense of humour of some minor KGB official. Now he knew that 'they' were prepared to deploy their top agents to destroy the best of games. As he had suspected from the beginning, as he had tried vainly to din into Hector Bootle's Whitehall-thickened head, there was a big fish behind friend Smirnov, a very big fish indeed. Who? Who?

Sitting here lost in thought in his favourite club armchair, virtually oblivious even to the fatal coronary of Sir Matthew Glossop, James Ball had been able to discern only the faintest outline of a solution. One thing was clear. He would need the Rover this afternoon for a journey north. The time had come to consult a better memory than his own.

17
MOLLY

Jan had released the Rover for the afternoon. The machine seemed to be grateful for its freedom. It was racing up the M I like a dog off the leash. A light drizzle, sufficient to keep the wipers in wheezing activity, was playing on the windscreen. The car's radio/casette was also playing – but not music. As he drove north, James Ball was listening once again to a recording made in Strangeways Prison of the interrogation of Umpire Peat

Peat: I've told you I don't know what the hell his game was!
Buster Tolchard (voice raised) : Come on you swine, you can do better than that. You jolly well better do better than that, or we'll break every bone in your body!
Peat: There's no need to turn nasty squire, I'm telling the truth . . . all right if you press me he did talk the once.
Tolchard: You better talk – and fast Peat.
Peat: Mind you it was a convivial occasion. We met one night over a couple of bottles of vodka in the old Grenadier in Baker Street. You could say tongues got loosened a bit; but I'm not quite sure I followed what Mr Smirnov was saying.
Tolchard: Sarn' Major, break this man's fingers, starting with the right index finger.
Sergeant Major: Sir!
Peat (loudly) : No! No please – not that finger. That right forefinger is my livelihood gentlemen. Break that and you destroy any chance I have to stand again.

Tolchard: Then you better spill it Peat!

Peat: He talked about a Professor Yakov, with some bitterness as I remember, sir. If I understood him correctly the gentleman is a lecturer in statistics with the KGB in Moscow. I got the impression he knew a lot about cricket for a Russian.

Tolchard: Impressions aren't good enough, you ugly ruffian. We want the facts.

Peat: . . . all the Test results since W.G. Grace and his gang.

Tolchard: Sarn' Major send for a double Scotch and set it down just out of this man's reach. I'm going to try a little 'carrot' with the 'stick'.

Peat: Now I'm remembering clearer. This professor has a bee in his bonnet.

Tolchard: Thank you Sarn' Major, just over there. Do you take it with soda or water, Peat? You can't have a drop of it with anything unless you try a bloody sight harder, you disgusting old criminal!

Peat: He has this theory, according to Mr Smirnov – something to do with cricket being connected with socio-ergonomics. . . .

Tolchard: Keep talking Peat.

Peat: My throat is horribly dry, sir. . . .

'A mad professor with a mad theory,' James Ball nodded dismissively as he poked the tape into silence. It was admittedly an explanation; but was it the *whole* explanation? 'There has to be another motive,' Bally whispered to the Northampton motorway exit.

A grey, damp day was closing early as Ball's Rover purred down Abington Avenue at the Football Ground End of the Northamptonshire County Cricket Ground. A dog barked as he stepped from the car in a parking site somewhere beyond the long on boundary and approached a caravan in which a candle was already burning.

A youngish woman was busy watering a row of potted tomato

plants as he drew near. She paused in her work to subject Ball to a hard, hostile stare.

'Oh God, it's you. Why can't you leave her alone?'

'I have to see Molly,' he answered bleakly.

'Don't stir it,' the girl spat at him, 'don't stir all those memories and records! Why don't you bloody well hop it back to London, and leave her in peace.'

'I have to pick her brain, if only for the last time,' he insisted.

'You're telling me it will be the last time if you start raking over these ashes again. Go back to London James Ball. You're not wanted here!'

Ball gently pushed past the now hysterical woman and stoopingly entered the dimly lit caravan. A hunched figure in a shawl was sitting over a guttering candle. The light was just good enough for the visitor to be able to observe that most of the remaining space was crammed with books and stationery. He noticed that the makeshift chair he was motioned to was in fact a stack of beige files stamped with the initials HMSO. Mementoes of Molly's long reign as Queen of the 'Oval's' files. Against the caravan's thin walls was a mountain of Wisdens. Ball felt a dull stab of guilt. The statistical history of the game was an interest they had shared, too passionately wagging tongues at the 'Oval' had hinted.

'Dear old Bally, you haven't changed,' the woman in the shawl chuckled as he set down a half bottle of Claymore whisky in front of her. 'Still the same mean old bastard!'

'Can I fetch you a mug, or would you prefer to drink it from the bottle?' he answered.

'Why stand on ceremony?' She coughed as she unscrewed the cap and put the half bottle to her lips. 'I lost any pretensions I had to be a lady long ago – as you well remember, Bally, you old sod.'

'Don't drink too much of it,' he cautioned, 'I want you to keep a clear head. We've got to go a long way together, Molly, a long way back into the records.'

'Old averages, old aggregates, old scores – my downfall . . .' she spluttered through a spasm of coughing. 'By the law of averages I should have died of them years ago.'

'Yellowfield,' Ball said. 'What can you tell me about Yellowfield?'

'Yellowfield, T. G. K.,' an activated human data bank recited. 'Eton, Cambridge and Worcestershire. Played for the Gentlemen v Players in 1937.'

'But never for England. Is that correct Molly?'

'No, and that was surprising, wasn't it, considering he scored 151 for the Gentlemen before he was stumped Ames bowled Goddard and, of course, the next week he went on to score 263 against Glamorgan – lbw Matthews if I remember right – the highest innings by an amateur batsman since the War. And don't forget England tried as many as nineteen players against New Zealand that year. They were experimenting with new talent in preparation for the Australian tour of 1938.'

'Who were the Test selectors that year, Molly?'

'Sir Pelham Warner, Sir Randolph Montgomery and Mr. K. W. Endcott-Spurling,' the oracle faultlessly replied.

Three selectors. One to die of natural causes, the second to lose a prized horse by Smirnov's hand at Goodwood in the summer of 1959, a year later, perhaps as a result, to suffer a fatal stroke; the third to meet with a terminal sailing accident off the coast of Albania, only last year, according to a Beaujolais-sodden MCC member. The pattern was becoming clearer.

'Afterwards, Molly. What happened afterwards to T. G. K. Yellowfield's career?'

'Well, of course he went to Spain, didn't he? I can't imagine he played much cricket there. Certainly it would have been difficult to fit in with reporting the Civil War from the Republican side.'

'What did the selectors have against Yellowfield?'

'I don't know, it's so long ago. And anyway who cares a fart?'

'Think Molly!'

'Rumours he was a bit too fond of this.' An arthritic hand clawed back the bottle. 'But then who can blame him? Whisky was three-and-six a bottle in those days. Even the pricey stuff, do you remember Bally? You used to buy me Johnnie Walker in those days! Oh you were a randy old one then my lad!'

'Yellowfield, Molly.'

'There was some talk of women – or was it boys? I don't remember. But then that's not unusual in cricket circles – women and boys, drugs and booze. There was something else . . . .'

'Politics?'

'That came later – no, an idea he didn't fancy the fast, short-pitched stuff. As I recall, the Selectors pointed to his poor showing against Larwood and Voce who, of course, were both going strong then, although "Lol" Larwood didn't play for England after the bodyline dust-up. It's true Yellowfield never did himself justice against Notts. I think you'll find he totalled only twelve in the two innings in the 1936 Worcestershire v Notts match and only nine in the 1937 encounter; but then he had a "retired hurt" in the second innings. I don't know if there was anything in it; but there's no doubt it rankled.'

'So much so that the name T. G. K. Yellowfield passes out of all the record books.'

'Yes, that was a little over-sensitive I thought – that deed-poll name change. He certainly showed he was no coward reporting the Civil War even if it was from the wrong side from the Establishment's point of view. Wounded, wasn't he, on the Aragon front?'

'Nevertheless T. G. K. Yellowfield becomes plain Tristan Field – Lieutenant Field – the "Oval's" most promising recruit of 1940.'

'He told me he never had liked the Yellow part of his name. Said they used to tease him at the Dragon School about it.'

'Plain Lieutenant Tristan Field,' Ball mused aloud, 'destined in the fullness of time to become Director of Counter Espionage and later Director-General of the "Oval" itself.'

'And then to leg it over to Moscow with half my files. I told you you should never have lent him my key!' Molly jabbed at the tender memories of times past.

Ball accepted the rebuke with an inclination of the head. The remnant carpeting on the caravan's floor seemed to have pictures on it. A picture of a young face under an officer's cap. Handsome features, fresh colouring, intelligent eyes, only a hint of mockery in the friendly smile. Then another face replaced it. The same face, in point of fact, but a craftier look in the eyes, a more emphatic distaste in the corner of the smile, and a nose become prematurely bulbous through a liking for strong drink. And then the mind's eye projected a third picture onto the carpet scraps. A photograph taken in a Moscow street. A haggard face under a fur cap wreathed in a smile of pure spite. KGB General Tristan Field. At last James Ball recognized his opponent!

'Going already Bally old boy?' Molly's rouged features now had an added flush. 'Time was when you'd find any old excuse to poke around my files. Couldn't stay away, could you my little Bally-bee. Remember?'

He kissed her briefly on the forehead. 'You've come up trumps as always,' he said. 'I must get back to London.'

'Zat all I get,' she slurred. 'No meeting of lips, no blending of hearts as the saying goes.' An explosion of earthy, choking laughter. She looked up at him with cataract crisscrossed, laughter, tragedy and whisky-soaked eyes. 'Don't look so nervous, Bally old fruit. All your secrets are safe with me. Even that old chestnut about you bowling the Nawab of Pataudi. *I won't tell a soul the Nawab of Pataudi was 238 not out, you lying old bugger!*' she thundered at a closing caravan door.

Molly's companion leapt at him out of the dusk like an embodiment of vengeance. The nozzle of a watering can grazed his cheek.

'Listen to her, you've really done it now!' She gesticulated towards the candle-lit caravan from which sounds of lachrymose singing were issuing. 'I'll have to go down to the off-licence and bring her a whole bottle of Bell's now. Thanks to your mean little gift, she'll be fighting drunk by midnight. Think what that's going to do to her, you stinking, sexist pig!'

Ball disengaged himself from the maddened woman and walked with slow dignity towards the parked Rover. The roar of abuse being hurled at his back was as nothing compared to the detonation that suddenly erupted in front of him. Ball flattened himself as the entire roof of the car whistled over his head and landed inches short of the screaming companion. A second volcanic explosion and what was left of the Rover became a towering inferno. I. Smirnov's time-bomb had been activated vital seconds too early, or too late.

18
HEADINGLEY

England were 21 for 6 wickets at lunchtime on the first day of the Third Test at Headingley and an England record of a kind. The lunch interval saw another record broken for the consumption of Samuel Smith's bitter.

Play resumed at ten minutes past two with a loudspeaker announcement, necessary perhaps in view of the crowd's unfamiliarity with the new England Caps, that Wally Ficket of Derbyshire and Larry Duck of Warwickshire were the not-out batsmen. In any case, it would have been difficult for even the most dedicated follower of the game to have made a positive identification of either player under the heavy weight of armour they were humping to the middle.

They were greeted with the roars and catcalls of a Roman amphitheatre for the entry of two particularly reluctant Christians. The third delivery of the afternoon session saw Larry Duck's off stump cartwheeling. He was replaced at the crease, as the loudspeaker patiently explained, by Neil Gnome of Gloucestershire.

'Happen he'll be the night watchman,' a spectator in front of James wisecracked.

'Bill Bowes woulder 'ad 'im for breakfast!' his elderly cloth-capped companion growled as Gnome weaved from a short-pitched riser. Over. The turn of Wally Ficket to face the bowling. The Derbyshire man had already betrayed a certain nervousness by making a headlong dash, at least as far as his padding would allow, to get to the non-striker's end off the last ball of the preceding over. However Gnome had firmly sent him back from the frying pan of a near run out to the fire of Jeff Thomson's hostile deliveries.

'Southern poofter!' snarled the elderly man in the cloth cap as Ficket flattened himself under a stump-skimming rocket. 'Derbyshire n'aint poofter,' his friend summoned sufficient impartiality to suggest. 'Poofters start at Watford Gap.'

'Poofters start a mile south of Sheffield and no lakey!' the cloth-capped Yorkshireman insisted. 'Take a look yonder!' Ficket had forced Neil Gnome into a suicidal run out. England were 22 for 8 wickets. Even the loudspeaker voice seemed drained of confidence as it announced that the incoming batsman was Gino Carstairs of Sussex.

'You'd 'ave thought they would have preferred Bairstow to Yon Friget!'

'Nay, never they!' Cloth Cap howled. 'This team is like all the rest – packed solid with poof and you know why? Because it's picked by a daft bugger from Harrow. Always has been, always will.'

'Least time we got two runs there,' the younger Yorkshireman commented as Carstairs cleared the slips with a lucky edge.

'What you mean "we" lad?' Cloth Cap demanded. 'They've now't to do with us – this Joe Soap's army!'

A thud like a boxer's fist hitting a punch ball. A shout like a convoy of flying pickets bursting a police cordon. Umpire Constant raised a sorrowful finger, and Gino Carstairs was trudging from the wicket.

'28 for 9. Thar's bloody risible,' said the younger man.

'Risible? It's a downright bloody disgrace!' Cloth Cap thundered. 'The biggest shower ever to play for England at Headingley – and they still can't find room for a Yorkshireman!'

'Abraham Udu of Glamorgan,' the loudspeaker announced.

But James Ball decided he had seen enough. Besides he was conscious that his Anthony Eden style homburg and 'British warm' overcoat were beginning to attract unfavourable attention. In the hostile glances of Cloth Cap and his compatriots

Ball sensed a lurking suspicion that his origins were somewhat south of the Watford Gap.

In fact he was relieved to have exited through the turnstile into St Michael's Lane when the roar went up which announced the fall of Abraham Udu's wicket.

England 29 all out was a score calculated to put a Headingley crowd in a mood to look for scapegoats.

'Your very good health, Hector,' Ball raised a glass of gin and tonic in the lounge of the Hotel Imperial, Leeds, 'This is indeed an unexpected kindness.'

'Why unexpected?' asked the Senior Security Adviser. 'Some people say I'm an extremely generous and spontaneous person.'

'I meant unexpected in the circumstances, Hector. I suspected you would feel I was somehow to blame for today's rather sorry performance.'

'England 29 all out. Australia 197 for no wicket. It's not much to write home about, is it?' Bootle laughed, out of the hysteria of despair, Ball assumed.

'You're going to ask me what I propose to do about it, Hector. Well what I propose to do about it is to offer you my resignation. You gave me until the Third Test to pull something off. It's quite clear that so far I have failed.'

'You mustn't take what I say too seriously, Bally old friend.' Bootle leaned across his double gin to pat the older man on the shoulder. 'You know I could never do without you, James. You're too good company. Particularly when it comes to sage advice on affairs of the heart. Cheers.'

Ball surfaced from an answering sip.

'In that case I better file my report, as it were. You see I haven't been exactly idle, nor exactly free of hazard, as my claim to the Civil Service Insurance Society for a new Rover will illustrate. But perhaps we could come to that later. First there's the immediate problem of L. M. S. Partridge. It's quite obvious that he and perhaps his committee have been tampered with – I suspect by an altogether more formidable operator than friend Smirnov, conceivably a woman.'

'Women, where would we be without them, eh!' Bootle raised a genial glass.

'Er. Yes. Well as I was about to suggest, Hector, it's imperative that Partridge is relieved of the Chairmanship of Selectors at once, however many strings have to be pulled. And this is a view I'm sure you'll want to represent to the Prime Minister in person.'

'Can't do anything about it next week. I'm taking a short holiday. Rented a cottage in the Lake District. Between you and me I won't be entirely alone.' Bootle winked.

Ball had never seen the senior civil servant in such a benign, not to say irresponsible mood. He wondered if it was the Yorkshire air. He had heard that it could be surprisingly invigorating.

'Listen James,' his old tormentor leaned forward to confide, 'you remember I told you a few months ago that my wife had left me for Australia.'

'The team or the country?'

'The country you old fool – no, at least I never had your problems. Anyway, I felt a bit down. Not that I missed her, you know. Just the feeling that she'd left it a bit late for any woman to want to look at me. Anyhow James, the most incredible thing has happened. I've met this absolutely gorgeous humdinger. I'm not joking. She'd make even you come out in a hot sweat, James. And the most fantastic thing of all is that I believe she rather fancies me. Have another double gin.'

'My congratulations Hector. Now if I could come to the second and more important item on my agenda. You know I've always said I'm convinced there's a very big fish behind this business. I believe,' his voice sank almost to inaudibility under the palm court orchestra's weeping strings, 'I've identified him. He is none other than our old friend. . . .'

'To the fair sex!' Bootle raised his freshened glass. 'God bless their pretty little socks! I'm sorry James, I didn't catch what you were saying.'

'It wasn't important,' Ball murmured. Something in Hector Bootle's exaggerated behaviour had suddenly alerted him to the danger of confiding in the Senior Security Adviser. He deliberately changed the subject. 'Tell me more about this paragon of female virtues.'

This was all the encouragement Bootle needed to burst into prolonged rhapsody. 'How can you possibly describe absolute perfection, James? Well, I'll have a shot at it. She's got the most gorgeous auburn hair which somehow reminds me of a Riviera sunset, utterly devastating green eyes and the most luscious pair of lips it's ever been my privilege to make the acquaintance of. I'm not one to insist on spectacular endowments, but the fact remains she's got an altogether glorious figure. And she certainly knows how to show it off to the most stunning effect. You see she's quite an unconventional little sweetie, James. She seldom wears anything more than a white scarf knotted across her bosoms and a pair of boy's shorts.

'But don't for heaven's sake get the idea that Melanie is just a gorgeous body, James. She's extremely sensitive and intelligent for a foreigner. Where's she from? Oh somewhere down Austria or the Balkans way. The accent is slightly German but there's nothing harsh about it. In fact if you want to know she's got a voice like an angel – a marvellous sexy angel! But as I was saying, she's no fool. For instance she knows an amazing amount about cricket for a foreigner – if you ask her she can give you the exact placing of every county in last year's championship table. And she's awfully clever about one's job and all that. She's got a wonderfully intuitive understanding of the sort of problems one has to face day in and day out. She's been a veritable gold mine of good advice on dealing with the Prime Minister. But then of course she has this incredible understanding of people, even people she's never met. I'm not saying she's always right. For instance it may surprise you to learn that she strongly recommends I should fire you, James. But most of the time she's bang on target. You're not going anywhere are you? I thought we were going to have dinner together. Really hammer the thing out you know, the whole fascinating question of this thing called Love.'

Ball had got to his feet and pointedly set his drained gin and tonic glass down on the plastic table. He also had an instinct about people. Now this instinct told him that his old friend Hector Bootle had fallen under the same sinister influence that had deranged the Chairman of Selectors.

'I'm sorry Hector,' he gazed down with a half-pitying smile at Bootle's florid face and bulbous love-blinded eyes, 'but I'm feeling a little tired. I really think I should turn in. I'm afraid,' he added meaningfully, 'that one way and another it's been a distressing day for England.'

A woman was standing at the window of his hotel bedroom. A tense figure silhouetted by the dim street lighting of Leeds drawing at the ghost of a cigarette. Ball turned the lights on, the woman's face turned from the window. He saw to his surprise that it was Jan and that she had been crying.

'Oh Bally,' she half sobbed, 'it's been such a terrible day.'

'I know,' he said. 'England 29 all out. Australia 197 for no wicket.'

'I'm afraid I haven't ever been very loyal to you, Bally,' she choked at the devastated heart of a once imposing Victorian gothic city. 'But you're always so good and tolerant, I feel I can confess to you. Bally, in all my life, I've never come across such a hopelessly green and inexperienced England team!'

19

MARKET PLACE

A busker in an Edwardian bathing costume was performing somersaults in fitful sunshine on the GLC's lovingly restored cobblestones. Not far from him the head of a man in an opera hat was noisily protruding from a wooden box flamboyantly labelled 'THE SMALLEST THEATRE IN THE WORLD'. Behind him the bells of St Paul's Covent Garden were tolling for another actor's memorial service.

They sat at a table at one of London's few open air cafés surrounded by tourists complaining in a variety of languages about the price of the drinks.

'I apologize for the venue, but I did not wish us to be conspicuous,' said I. Smirnov. 'Personally I find this new Covent Garden complex very artificial and plastic. If one must go anywhere in this decadent city I prefer the more traditional drinking establishments.'

Smirnov's companion was a young woman. This much was clear from the slim bronzed hand on the stem of her Pernod glass and the full lips to which, from time to time, it was being raised. Whether she was beautiful or not was uncertain. Her face was almost completely masked by a combination of an upturned mackintosh collar and an immense pair of dark glasses.

'Perhaps you are becoming tired of London,' she said. 'Perhaps it is time for you to go home.'

'Home?' Smirnov smiled dismissively. 'How can I go home

when there is still so much work to do here?'

'The Third Test Match has been lost by England by an innings and 391 runs. They will lose the next Test Match by a similar margin. I have arranged that, too. I cannot see that there is work to detain you, comrade. The mission can be safely left in my hands.'

Smirnov reddened. 'My instructions from Supreme Control specifically state that you are to liaise closely with me. Although not explicitly stated, a careful reading of my instructions can leave no doubt but that in all essential respects you are attached to me – you are under my orders.'

'And my instructions make it quite clear that you have failed entirely in your mission, comrade. You have not succeeded in losing for England even one Test. Also you have been drawing attention to yourself by absurd acts of sabotage and infantile assassination attempts. If you wish me to be brutally candid, my instructions are saying I am to avoid all contacts with your operation and report directly to Ultimate Control.'

I. Smirnov was rapidly beginning to lose his curiosity about the face behind the dark glasses. In fact he was no longer interested whether it was attractive or ugly; he had come to the conclusion he had seldom met a woman he more cordially disliked. He showed an imperfect set of teeth.

'You know what you are saying is Cult-of-the-Individual idiocy. Control knows that my contacts in England are too important to be ignored – they include the whole of the Counter-Espionage organization, MI5 – codeword the "Oval".'

'MI5? Their cover has been blown for over thirty years.' Stephanie smiled pityingly. 'Besides what do they know about cricket? Mr L. M. S.. Partridge, the Chairman of the Test Selectors, he is the power in cricket, and now he is asking me to marry him, on his knees.'

'That side for the Third Test Match – it was, let us be honest, so obvious,' I. Smirnov fired back with a salvo of genuine Muscovite bitchery. 'So obvious that this Porridge has been compromised by some boy or prostitute. It was so obvious it is certain to alert the security forces still loyal to Mrs

Thatcher, certain to provoke retaliation from men like Mr Hector Bootle and the notorious spycatcher Mr James Ball.'

'Mr Hector Bootle is waiting for me now in a cottage in the Lake Districts,' Stephanie answered crushingly. 'He was hoping to spend the whole week with me, but a whole week would not be good for a man of his age. Besides tonight I am to have dinner with the Minister of Sport. Next week I am to be introduced to Mr James Ball.' She added without a hint of arrogance, 'He will be bowled over by my methods, not yours.'

'The phrase is "bowlered out",' Smirnov corrected her sharply. 'How reliable is your knowledge of cricket, comrade?'

'Lionel Partridge wishes me to play for the Women of England versus the Women of New Zealand at Lord's,' the loathsome woman once more snubbed him.

On a warmish July evening in Covent Garden, I. Smirnov experienced an unwelcome return to past times. An afternoon in a blizzard on a railway platform on the Soviet-Chinese border, a numb groping for the warming vodka hip flask, only to find it had turned to ice. On the face of it, a meaningless memory; but its point was not lost on Smirnov himself. If this despicable female was given a free rein he would be back in Russia within a week, back on the Soviet-Chinese border, or, worse, dead – unless death was preferable to the Soviet-Chinese border. He decided on a new approach. Somehow he had to make this scarily efficient woman his friend.

'Please to join me in another drink,' he gestured with a show of affability. 'You know it is so long since I am talking with anyone from our side. It can be a little lonely, you know. Lonely because there is not anybody with whom to share one's thoughts.'

'I am trained to have no thoughts,' Stephanie answered unhelpfully, 'and in no circumstances to share them.'

'Nevertheless you must sometimes have thought to yourself what can be the purpose of our mission.'

'My mission?'

'To risk imprisonment, disgrace, perhaps death in the cause of a theory, the theory of a professor of statistics called Yakov who wears his grey hairs as long as a dissident's. To bring all our experience of subversion and anarchy-creation against what is fundamentally only a game – you must sometimes have wondered, when you are alone at night, comrade, have our superiors gone crazy?'

'I am never alone at night,' Stephanie replied flatly.

Try a sexual overture, Smirnov suggested to himself. After all, if the woman was to be believed, there had to be an extremely desirable personality behind the disguise of the dark glasses and the extensive mackintosh. 'I know an agent is not expected to have opinions; but in my view a woman of your skills could be so much more effectively employed on behalf of our Soviet Rupublics than to be infiltrating what is only a version of *lapta* played with six sticks. It is evident to me that a woman with your capabilities, comrade, could easily bring down the fascist Tory government, disorientate the Cruise missile programme, secure the United Kingdom's withdrawal from Europe – even persuade it into a declaration of war against the United States.'

Smirnov's switch to unashamed flattery was arguably beginning to work. At least a suspicion of a smile was beginning to form on the full lips at the Pernod glass's rim. Possibly he was too encouraged. 'Together,' he ventured, 'we can help one another to make sense of our crazy orders, whisper to each other the secrets that we dare not share with the class enemy.' At the same time he slid his hand under the mackintosh and began a rapid exploration towards the thighs. That was all he remembered of his sexual overture. The next thing I. Smirnov knew was that he was somersaulting like the busker in an Edwardian bathing costume across the GLC's lovingly restored cobblestones.

She passed him as he was sitting up to rub his head, a karate expert in a black mackintosh moving with undulating hips towards King Street. She turned round before she was out of earshot. 'You are too tired and too old for any games,' she hissed. 'You should go home before you are ordered home.'

She was approaching Moss Bros when I. Smirnov finally

picked himself up, dusted off his suit and reclaimed his trilby.

'You cannot get shot of me so easily you Bavarian bitch!' he bellowed after her. 'You wait. You see, I will kill James Ball before you can get to him. I will be true to my orders. Long before you, I will blow your flanelled imbeciles to small pieces!'

20

WHO SELECTS THE SELECTORS?

A few yards away James Ball was lunching in the Garrick Club. Laurence Olivier was eating at the next table. Sir John Gielgud was seated by the window. In the centre of the dining room Sir Hugh Casson and Peter Ustinov were in animated conversation.

'I thought it best to meet somewhere quiet where we don't know anybody,' Ball explained *sotto voce* to his guest. 'There are certain rather delicate matters I need to discuss, informally of course, Sir Godfrey.'

'I've never lunched at the Garrick,' said Lieutenant General Sir Godfrey Crater. 'I must say the consommé is excellent, well worth the journey.'

'I'm afraid it is a little way from Lord's.'

'Long way from anywhere isn't it? Never mind, the sherry is excellent.'

'And it's really Lord's and matters pertaining thereunto that I wanted to sound you about.' Ball took a firmer hold on the conversational rudder, for it was in his role as a power behind the scenes in the highest echelons of cricket administration that Sir Godfrey needed to be consulted.

'Lots of things happening in Covent Garden I hear,' said the retired General who had other interests than cricket. 'New property developments going on, new banks going up, all splendid.'

'It must be vexing for you and the Committee to have to contend with all this criticism, not unjustified in my view, of the Chairman.'

'We've never been able to sort out the management of ICI properly,' Sir Godfrey conceded. 'We have the same trouble with British Petroleum and Marks & Spencer. This country doesn't seem to produce leaders any longer.'

'I was referring,' Ball dropped his voice to a level where it could just be heard through Casson and Ustinov's exchange of pleasantries, 'to the Chairman of the Test Selectors.'

'Oh, yes that. Leaving his wife, isn't he? Always unsettles a fellow a bit. Suspect he'll shake out of it.'

'Sir Godfrey, we cannot afford a repetition of Headingley,' James Ball asserted softly.

'Oddly enough the gate receipts were rather encouraging, considering the match only went to the fourth morning. Nobody can quite account for it. Unless,' the General's neat, grey moustache raised its wings in a brief smile, 'you can put it down to Yorkshire relish at seeing an England team take a bit of a knock.'

The fish pie arrived. James Ball signalled forward the chilled Pouilly Fuisse.

'The fish pie is a bit of a speciality at the Garrick,' he remarked with a club man's instinct for the moment when conventional courtesies must elbow commerce aside.

'Well you're quite near the sea down here, aren't you?' Sir Godfrey answered. 'Nice plonk, by the way.'

'If I may talk business for a moment, Sir Godfrey, I must tell you, in the strictest confidence, that there are security reasons, as well as the obvious consideration of national interest, why L. M. S. Partridge should be immediately removed from the Chairmanship of the Test Selectors.'

'Remove the incumbent in mid-season?' The retired General paused while he picked a fishbone from his mouth. 'I'm not sure it's ever been done. I'm not even sure it *can* be done.'

'May I be bold enough to enquire why?' Ball refilled his guest's glass.

'It might have been easier in the old days when the powers that be were just a few of us on the MCC Committee; but now we've got this Test and County Cricket Board set up. That's rather a different kettle of fish,' Sir Godfrey added after removing another bone.

'It's always been something of a mystery to me – the question of who exactly selects the Selectors. Sir Godfrey, for security reasons it it now becoming imperative that I find the answer.'

'There's no pat answer,' Ball's luncheon guest assured him. 'Strictly speaking it's the Test and County Cricket Board.'

'Then presumably I will have to approach them,' Ball said, betraying a latent bulldog streak. 'England really cannot afford another Headingley.'

'You'll have a business getting them all together; because, of course, they include representatives of the seventeen first-class counties, the CCC and the major minor counties. As far as I know they're not due to meet again until October and you can understand why in a way. Costs a small fortune in charabancs.'

From the walls of the Garrick Club dining room Edmund Keane, dressed for the part of Richard III, looked down with an expression of malevolent despair. Ball refilled his distinguished guest's glass sombrely. 'Do I take it that the MCC has no influence over the process of the selection of the Selectors?'

'Not officially. We've been advised to keep a low profile, ever since some of our out-of-town Members started roughing up the umpires in the Centenary Test.'

'Unofficially then?' James Ball persisted.

'Superficially no, but behind the scenes – and I'm speaking strictly off the record of course – we're still able to make our views felt.'

'They do a very good bread and butter pudding here,' Ball said, noting that his guest's plate was clean, except for a neat pile of fishbones. 'Or would you rather have the gorgonzola?' Without waiting for the answer he rapped out, 'In any case, Sir Godfrey, are you prepared to use your no doubt considerable influence behind the scenes to get Partridge dismissed before he announces another disastrous team next Sunday morning?'

Patrick Moore was talking to Robert Morley about his bowling action. Donald Sinden was entertaining a BBC producer with a few speeches from his forthcoming TV play, Peter Ustinov was telling Sir Hugh Casson about a recent gastronomic tour of Bulgaria. All of them were silenced by the urgent and anxious tone in which this question was couched.

'I'll try the bread and butter pudding,' Sir Godfrey answered. 'As far as the other business goes, I'm afraid I'm going to be rather tied up for the next week or so. Flying to Hong Kong tomorrow. See if we can calm them down about the Chinese takeover. If you like, I'll take a few soundings when I get back.'

From a gilt frame the actor-manager Sir Henry Beerbohm Tree, dressed for the part of Hamlet's stepfather, Claudius, looked down doubtfully from his prayers.

'Sir Godfrey by the time you get back from Hong Kong the game will have been brought into further disrepute by another humiliating defeat for a risible England Eleven. Who knows? Perhaps the twelve for the final Test will already have been selected.'

'The trouble is, as I hinted earlier, there are no established procedures for removing a sitting Chairman of Selectors, even if as you suggest the fellow's blotted his copy book with you people. Under this TCCB set-up the machinery just isn't there. It's something I will have to raise at the next annual meeting in January.'

'By January we will be touring Australia with a Third, perhaps even a Fourth England Eleven,' Ball suggested with a candour of feeling that surprised him. 'By the way they do a very good Italian brandy here,' he added, hastily recalling himself to his duties as a host, clubman and mandarin.

'I'll have an armagnac if that's all right. If I may say so, I don't think you fully appreciate how things have changed in the game recently. Time was for instance when a word in the right ear could get an England captain stood down overnight – remember that fellow Close, and Chapman for that matter. But now it's all been "democratized", as they say, at least officially.

You've got to put your word in a hell of a lot of quite frankly pretty hairy ears.'

'Of course: the representatives of the seventeen first-class counties, the CCC and the major minor counties.' Ball gave a resigned nod. 'You know, Sir Godfrey, I'm beginning to wonder how this body ever managed to get around to selecting a Chairman of Selectors in the first place.'

'A good question,' his guest conceded. 'I must raise it at the AGM in January.'

A few minutes later, Ball was escorting Sir Godfrey down the long flight of steps that leads from the acme of artistic achievement into the light of common day, Garrick Street.

'Thank you for lunch,' his guest said. 'I've enjoyed picking up the threads again from whenever it was. Mustn't leave it so long next time.'

'One final question, Sir Godfrey.' Ball smiled tensely, his hand gripped the banister for restraint rather than support. 'You haven't by any chance run into an attractive foreign girl recently? Auburn hair like a Riviera sunset? Simple white scarf knotted across her breasts? Surprisingly well-informed about cricket?'

'Certainly not,' the retired General answered tartly. 'And quite frankly, nobody asks a gentleman questions like that at my clubs!' The umbrella he raised for a taxi went up like a sword.

You're losing your cool, Ball. You're losing your nerves. You're losing your legendary subtlety, James told himself as he walked disconsolately towards Leicester Square tube station. And who else was there to tell him but himself? James Ball was a man alone, carrying what felt like the weight of all England on his shoulders.

21

THE PARTY FOR NOTTINGHAM

As if alerted by James Ball's behind-the-scenes activities, the Chairman of Selectors broke with precedent by announcing the squad for the Fourth Test Match on Wednesday instead of the traditional Sunday morning. In fact he had no dramatic changes to announce. The team which had been routed at Headingley was retained with only one substitution. Wally Ficket of Derbyshire was replaced behind the stumps by Denis Dove, Leicestershire's reserve keeper. The announcement produced other 'firsts' for cricket – the resignation of two of the Chairman's fellow Selectors, an unprecedented occurrence, at least in mid-season, and the appearance of L. M. S. Partridge before the cameras as first item on both BBC and ITN News.

'You can't work miracles overnight,' he explained to his tense interrogators. 'We're in the business of radical change, and that takes a little time before you see positive results. Please don't interrupt me. I am well aware that some of the lads performed below expectation at Headingley. But don't let's forget that for many of them – indeed for all of them – it was their first Test. No, you've asked me a question, allow me to answer it. Of course we could play safe and field established names and mature talents; but let me make it quite clear that this Selection Committee is committed to youth.

'Don't interrupt. You asked me a question and I propose to answer it. I am well aware of the resignations in my Committee. There are always people who are going to drag their feet when it comes to radical change, people who find the pace of revolutionary selection frankly too hot for them. That's their problem. We're in the business of blooding youth and vigour.

'Please don't try and interrupt. The short answer is no, I don't necessarily expect this team to win the Trent Bridge Test, though naturally we will be very pleasantly surprised if they do. Let me make it quite clear we're looking at broader horizons than Trent Bridge and even the Oval. You asked me a question please be good enough to hear me out. In fact, let me give you an analogy. I believe that English cricket can be compared to a reasonably successful man approaching his middle years. Increasingly he finds himself falling a little short in performance, both at work and at play. Increasingly he's inclined to dwell on past glories, regard the present as a matter of mere humdrum routine. Then he meets someone – let's say a woman – much younger than himself, fresh and beautiful beyond his wildest dreams. Suddenly the world looks bright and new. He forgets the worries about the wrinkles on his forehead and the children's public school fees. He feels restored, effective, wanted, loved. In the arms of a young instructress he undergoes amazing changes.

'Now that in a nutshell is what I am trying to do for English cricket. Please don't interrupt me and in any case I resent your insinuation. As I was saying, it is no accident that every member of my Twelve for Trent Bridge is under twenty-five. It's no accident because I passionately believe that only from the embrace of red-blooded youth can English cricket hope to rediscover its ardour and virility.'

Ball walked stiffly to the television set – Jan kept the remote control model upstairs – and blackened the screen.

'Damned fellow ought to be put up against a wall,' Buster Tolchard growled.

'"And all for love," Buster, as Dryden said.' James gave his young associate a twisted smile. 'Or do you prefer Shakespeare? – "Oh what eyes hath love put in my head."' He decided from Tolchard's expression of bemused indignation that the ex-phone tapper read little poetry, even of the anthology kind. Perhaps it was just as well. He needed Buster, not for his intellect but for his simple, unsophisticated patriotism. All the more so because just now that quality had become as rare as a Raphael sonnet, as Browning might have put it.

'I'm buggered if I'm going to watch the next Test Match, even on TV,' Buster was saying. 'I'm damned if I'm going to be made ashamed to be English again.'

'Don't worry Buster. You won't be anywhere near the Fourth Test Match. You're going to Moscow.'

Tolchard began a low whistle which ended on a piercing note. 'Moscow! But that's enemy territory.'

'I'm sorry that with things the way they are, I can't promise you too comfortable a ride. To be candid, Buster, I don't want anyone to know about this trip. Between you and me I've got to fiddle this one on my own, rather limited expenses. I'm afraid that's going to mean a cut-rate Intourist package with accommodation at one of Moscow's lesser-known hotels.'

'I don't want to bind, Sir; but there are quite a few nasty pieces of work back in Moscow with scores to settle with yours truly. Is there any chance you could send someone else?'

'There is no one else, Buster,' Ball stated grimly. 'No one else I can trust,' he elaborated with a sigh.

'What do you want me to do in Moscow?' Tolchard reached for the reassurance of his briar pipe.

'You will meet a man – quite an important man in certain Moscow circles – and ask him a question.'

'What question, Sir?'

'It's very simple,' Ball smiled delphically. 'You will ask him what he remembers of the English cricket season of 1937.'

'Well,' Tolchard said after a moment or two's reflection. 'I suppose I better be going – start sorting out my effects for Moscow. I wonder if it's still snowing over there.' He got to his feet shaking the pipe tobacco strands off his tweed trousers. At the door he turned to ask with a half-apologetic, half-accusatory frown, 'What are you going to do about this rodent Partridge in the meantime?'

'I am going to see the Prime Minister,' Ball answered. 'I'm due in Downing Street at eleven tomorrow morning.'

22

BATTING AT NUMBER TEN

'I hope there are no misunderstandings about this audience I have granted you, Mr Ball,' the Prime Minister said. 'I am not looking to make any additions to my staff of senior security advisers at present.'

James lowered a thinning grey head. 'Quite so Ma'am.'

'If anything I am looking for manpower savings in this area.'

'Unfortunately that may become necessary,' he answered, as the flushed and infatuated face of Hector Bootle swam into his mind's eye.

'I confess I am a little uncertain as to what I owe this pleasure,' the Prime Minister announced. Her usually sensitive ears had missed the tone of mildly dramatic assertion in James Ball's voice. 'To be perfectly frank my knowledge of you is somewhat limited. I know that my senior security advisers sometimes find it necessary to bring you out of retirement on a freelance basis. Again I seem to remember your name has cropped up in connection with the Honours List – some question about the suitability of ladyship for Mrs Ball if I remember right. In any case, what can I do for you Mr Ball, bearing in mind that my time is extremely valuable?'

'Prime Minister I have to tell you that England is facing annihilating defeat.'

'That is not my information,' the steely supremo replied tartly. 'From Buenos Aires to Bonn I believe that people are beginning to understand that Britain means business.'

'I was talking of cricket, Prime Minister.'

'I don't have much time for cricket. In that way I'm like the Queen.'

'However Ma'am, I have to report that our enemies are interested in cricket,' Ball stolidly countered, 'interested in the total destruction of the English game.'

'Mr Bootle was trying to waste my time with this absurd theory some weeks ago,' the PM confided after reflection. 'I'm glad to say we've heard no more about it recently.'

'Precisely for the reason that Hector Bottle has fallen, temporarily at least, prey to the malign influence of a female KGB agent,' James explained with a pained smile. It was impossible not to feel in a sense that ran deeper than politics and national loyalties that he was betraying a friend, or if not a friend an associate in high places.

'Have you any evidence for this extraordinary allegation?' the Premier snapped.

James Ball had heard it whispered on the grapevine that strong spirits were not totally debarred from Number Ten Downing Street. Now he found his eyes ransacking the tasteful Adam and Chippendale appointments for the slightest hint of a concealed cocktail cabinet. The truth was that Ball, though not an intemperate man, had never felt more in need of a strong gin and tonic.

'Hector Bootle is normally the most discreet of officials,' he heard his voice struggle on in a dry, teetotal tone not of his choosing. 'My understanding is that he has recently been confiding recklessly to this woman.'

'That's still not hard and fast evidence.'

'One example may help to illustrate my thesis, Ma'am. It appears that Hector Bootle has taken this creature so far into his confidence as to allow her to advise him on his appointments. I gather,' Ball blushed, 'that she has gone so far as to recommend my dismissal.'

'Who is this unusual woman?' the PM enquired with a noticeable awakening of interest.

'We have yet to make a positive identification Ma'am; but you can see her handiwork in the selection of the farcical team that will represent England at Trent Bridge next Thursday.'

'It's the same team that lost by all those runs in Yorkshire isn't it?'

'Almost exactly Ma'am, and it will lose by a similar catastrophic margin in Nottingham.'

'And you say you can detect a woman's hand in all this as well?' The Premier was no longer looking both busy and bored.

'The same Delilah who has, so to speak, shorn Hector Bootle's hair. Of that I am convinced,' James declared.

The Prime Minister pushed back her gilt chair and walked with unsteady steps towards the window. It was true she had bought a new pair of high-heeled shoes at Harrods that morning; but the news James Ball had to impart was not such as to contribute to the Leader's equilibrium.

'Why?' she asked a milling crowd of tourists in the narrow, heavily-policed street below. 'Why on earth should our enemies go to all these lengths to sabotage a game, a pretty uninteresting game in my view?'

Salisbury, Campbell Bannerman, Asquith, Lloyd George, MacDonald, Chamberlain, Churchill, Eden, Macmillan, Heath . . . Ball mentally recited all the Prime Ministers of this country who had likewise found the game uninteresting. He reflected with a stab of sadness that had there been rather more enthusiasm for cricket at the top, the course of the twentieth century might have been different.

But these were reflections to be pursued at a less anxious time, perhaps in the company of an erudite friend in the shade of the Pavilion's upper tiers during some slumberous county match on a balmy afternoon at Lord's when cricket had finally been rescued from the dark clouds that hung over it. Then there would also be time to theorize about that short list of Prime Ministers who had actually espoused the game – Baldwin, Douglas Home, Attlee and Wilson, Conservative and Labour equally divided. Had not an accident of history placed Sir Alec in brief occupation of Number Ten, Labour would have had an unexpected majority. No, these were not matters to discuss with a busy Conservative Prime Minister who was looking at him with eyes which signalled a stern request for guidance.

'The explanation may sound incredible to you, Prime Minister,' he bluntly stated, 'but I believe it lies in the fact that a Worcestershire batsman called T. G. K. Yellowfield was not invited to play for England in the season of 1937.'

'I've told you I'm not well informed about cricket.' The note of impatience had returned to the First Lady's voice.

'You will know him better as Tristan Field, Ma'am, lately of the "Oval", presently of the KGB.'

Suddenly the austere figure at the window was a vulnerable, trembling woman, 'I don't want to hear that name in my presence!' she shrilled. 'I refuse to be accountable for other Prime Minister's moles. Do I make myself clear? I've had to deal with quite enough Parliamentary questions about Mr Field and his friends in high places ever to want to hear him mentioned again!'

The crucial moment in the interview had arrived. James was strongly tempted, in view of the fiery glances which were being directed towards him, to change the subject, at least temporarily; return to the attack by a more roundabout, less mine-strewn route. But in his heart he knew it had never been more imperative to stick to his guns.

'I fear there will be many more Parliamentary questions raised concerning KGB General Field, Ma'am, if we do not act with the utmost urgency to foil his latest game,' he asserted.

'What do you want me to do?' Superficially the tone was harsh and waspish, but Ball did not miss the note of entreaty which underlay it.

'Prime Minister, I believe I may have a plan to "catch and bowl" Mr Field, hopefully once and for all. However it will take time to mature, and it will require the fullest co-operation of your Government. Meanwhile we have a Test series to draw, even if we cannot now hope to win.'

'Go on Mr Ball,' the Prime Minister nodded with a hint of approval.

'It is obviously too late, were it even feasible, to persuade the

Chairman of Selectors to reconsider his party for the Fourth Test Match at Nottingham. No, all we can hope for in this department is to secure his resignation before the team for the Fifth Test Match is announced, and here as with so many facets of this operation I must look to you Ma'am to provide the necessary pressure. This still leaves us with the problem of the Fourth Test. If we lose at Nottingham we forfeit all hope of squaring the series and retaining the "Ashes". I am sure I do not need to remind you, limited as your time is for cricket, Ma'am, what a baleful effect the loss of yet another Test series particularly against the old enemy, Australia, would have on the nation's morale. There is of course no hope whatsoever of winning at Nottingham; but there is just a chance with a little favour from fortune that we could force a draw.'

'I don't see how I can be of any help in all this.' The Prime Minister was beginning to look beadily busy again.

'Only you can make a draw possible, Your Majesty,' Ball assured her with a slip of the tongue which just could have been intentional. 'Awaiting trial at this moment in Strangeways Prison is a former tool of the KGB called Umpire Reg Peat. From the enquiries I have made I am convinced it will be possible to "turn" this agent to England's advantage. But first Peat will require an immediate Royal pardon. I hope you understand why I had to come to you.'

'That's easily arranged.' The Prime Minister moved with a confident stride back to her gilt chair and writing desk. 'Now, Mr Ball,' she smiled, 'tell me about your plans for putting that unspeakable Mr Field in the bag. . . .'

It was becoming uncomfortable on the roof of Number Eleven Downing Street, traditional home of the Chancellor of the Exchequer. It would of course have been easier without the encumbrance of a specialist rifle from the Kalashnikov armoury, itself encumbered with telescopic sights and silencer. But then I. Smirnov's whole reason for being there was assassination, accurate and discreet.

He had observed his human target enter the front door of

Number Ten – too late to get the slightly stooping head neatly in his sights. He had not despaired. His prey was notorious; but his rank in the British Establishment was unlikely to obtain him more than a ten-minute audience, or so I. Smirnov had reasoned.

But the minutes and then the quarter hours were dragging by. And now Big Ben was tolling noon with the raucousness of a battery of Chinese field guns. Why Chinese field guns? Because I. Smirnov's thoughts had once again returned to the discomforts of the Sino-Soviet border – discomforts far more acute and ultimately soul-destroying than the roof of the Chancellor of the Exchequer's official residence. This was why he had to wait. Why, when his target finally presented itself, he could not afford to miss. The old Englishman had to die, here in the privileged confines of Downing Street, before Agent Stephanie could reach him. The aged and eccentric nymphomaniac Jan Ball had to be widowed, if only to disprove a loathsome woman's contention that he was due for recall.

Now! The policemen on duty in the street below were springing to attention, touching their helmets. The old man had shuffled onto the pavement outside the First Minister's residence. Smirnov brought the rifle up with a savage tug, tearing, in the process, a tile from the Chancellor of the Exchequer's roof. He froze as the tile slid menacingly down the sloping roof. Then lodged with a dull clunk in the drainpipe. No police faces turned upwards. Hold the rifle steady. Yes, that's the picture you want. The balding grey head was filling his sights like an obliging balloon. Steady the intersection of the cross on the temples. Wait, your hair is getting in the way. No, it's not your hair. Your hair is sandy grey. This hair is blonde-coloured and sparklingly radiant.

Smirnov raised his eyes from the telescope. A woman was effectively masking the old man. He searched furiously for another angle. The old man's umbrella was the only extremity in view. And now a Government car had drawn up to the pavement. The woman was shaking the old man by the hand. Now? No, she had leaned forward to help him into the back seat of the car, as solicitously as a daughter. And now the door had been closed and the car was speeding away in the direction of Whitehall. Take a chance at a shot through the rear window? No, the woman was blocking his view of the rear window, standing there waving. His finger started to tighten vindictively on the trigger. Then it reluctantly relaxed. I. Smirnov's orders had been ambiguous in some respects; but in one matter they had been clear and categorical. No diplomatic incidents! No attempt on Government Ministers – least of all on the British First Minister, on pain of liquidation!

How could I. Smirnov have foreseen, how indeed could James Ball himself have forseen, that the Prime Minister would do him the exceptional honour of accompanying him onto the pavement of Number Ten to offer him the use of her personal car?

In a spasm of frustrated fury Smirnov took aim at a perching bird on a nearby chimney-pot and fired a silenced shot. A Brazilian tourist in the Horse Guards Parade was surprised to find that an exploded pigeon had landed at his feet.

23

AN ENGLISHMAN ABROAD

Buster Tolchard wished he had brought another suit. He was sweating profusely under his tweed. He suspected, from the number of times he felt impelled to bend down and scratch, that he was developing a heat rash around the knees. Clearly the Muscovites understood their weather better than his travel agent. The women were wearing summer frocks. The men had light-weight suits or had discarded their jackets to display short-sleeve open neck shirts and braces. Many were wearing knotted handkerchiefs as sunhats. Through the trees of Gorky Park, Tolchard could see two dumpy girls suntanning themselves in one-piece bathing costumes.

A burning blue sky, as unrelenting as Russia's plains, had riveted itself onto the minarets of Moscow. Even here in the park the heat was as suffocating as an African capital. Tolchard longed to throw off his tweed jacket and tear loose his Old Harrovian tie (he was, in reality, an Old Brightonian). But that would have been contrary to instructions. His contact had been told to look for a man wearing an Old Harrovian tie carrying a copy of the *Daily Telegraph*.

In the winter it provided a steel hard surface for skaters. This afternoon it was choppy with rowing boats and noisy with the shouts of children. Here on the south side of the Gorky Park lake, by the footpath intersection, was the rendezvous. Tolchard consulted his watch and noted he was still ten minutes early. Time for a paddle? Now he was fighting an impulse to take off his walking shoes and woollen socks and sink his feet into cooling lake water. He finally surrendered to the impulse. He laid his shoes and socks by a nearby plane tree and advanced towards the water's edge. Here he paused to inspect a sign in Russian which may or may not have read 'Paddling Prohibited'. It was an expensive pause, because suddenly Tolchard felt a blow in the small of his back, as if from a charging bull. With maximum propulsion he was rocketed into the water.

The shock of the blow and the unexpected dive slowed Tolchard's reactions. He swallowed dangerous quantities of muddy, urban lakewater. Then he started to overreact. Working his arms with a violent pumping motion he succeeded only in steering himself further away from shore and a firm foothold. The sign in Russian had warned would-be paddlers of the surprising depth of the lake at this point.

Now Tolchard was fighting against the dead weight of his suit as well as a drastic shortage of breath. Briefly his head broke the lake's filmy surface. A vague impression of blue sky. Circling boats and the imminence of death by suction. He made the mistake of trying to call for help before his mouth was clear and swallowed further choking quantities of murky liquid. Now his head went under again. Delightful but dangerous images started to float through his mind – the rugby fields at Brighton College, a certain prefect in cricket flannels he had once secretly worshipped, a girl smiling at him across a Young Conservative ballroom. Tolchard's life, or its brighter moments, was passing before his eyes.

The classics and their mythology had been beaten into Tolchard at his preparatory school and later driven home by subtler methods at Brighton College. For this reason, as he neared the shores of extinction, he was perhaps half expecting a Ferryman. He saw him first through veils of water. A lean hook-nose figure bent over his oar in a similar attitude to Father Time leaning over the stumps at the Grand Stand at Lord's. It might be Charon's craft but at least it would be dry, Buster reasoned as he clawed himself aboard with a drowning man's vigour. Now he was face to face with an elderly man wearing a

Panama hat, white trousers and a Free Forester blazer, and a not altogether charitable smile.

'I apologize,' the Ferryman finally spoke. 'Vasili can sometimes be a little playful. And, of course, he has never played cricket. But then I think you've met before. At "the cage" in Harpenden. I understand from Vasili that you didn't play cricket either, Mr Tolchard.'

'Where am I?' Buster gasped.

'Enjoying a row on the lake in Gorky Park, having survived, if I may say so, from a rather inept effort at bathing which incidentally is strictly prohibited in this part of the lake. Thank you Vasili!' He nodded towards the shore. Under the plane tree where Tolchard had parked his shoes and socks a thickset man was grinning evilly in their direction. Even at this distance, Buster was able to recognize the former Fourth Cultural Attaché to the Soviet Embassy in Kensington. The boot had been on the other foot then – at least at 'the cage' in Harpenden.

'I want to be taken to my embassy!' Buster announced calmly but firmly.

'Oh don't be a chump,' the Ferryman chided. 'You've come all this way to see me. And anyway there's so much to talk about. Whole seasons to talk about.'

Buster made a closer inspection of his Ferryman host. 'T. G. K. Yellowfield!' he finally exclaimed.

'Field, if you don't mind, Mr Tolchard, Tristan Field. And please don't bother to call me General, it's an awfully common title in this country.' He shipped his oars and held out his hand, a hand as white and withered as an ancient pianist's.

'I'm afraid I don't shake hands with traitors,' Tolchard told him.

'Never mind,' the former Third Man smiled thinly. 'I suppose by the way you didn't bring any Craven 'A' cigarettes with you. You just can't get them out here. Oh I'm sorry,' he eyed Tolchard's soaked tweed jacket. 'Even if you had brought some, they wouldn't be exactly smokable, would they? But tell me about England. How is Wystan Auden and Cyril Connolly? And dear old Walter Hammond. Oh I forgot – they're all dead aren't they?'

'I've never heard of them, except for Hammond that is,' Tolchard suddenly confessed.

'Pity about old Walter – such a wonderful off-drive, such a chump with women. You know I could never understand how he persuaded that bunch of holier than thou old blimps to make him captain of England. I mean look what they did to poor old Percy Chapman, just because his father owned a brewery and he got bored with wallop. Talking of Percy I don't suppose you've brought a bottle of Dimple Haig with you? I haven't tasted the stuff in years. Never mind. How's Percy Fender? How's dear old Harold Macmillan? How's Len Hutton and Cyril Washbrook? How's poor old Stephen Spender and Alan Ross and Grantchester? Is there honey still for tea?' the KGB General enquired.

'I don't suppose you have a drop of cognac on you?' Buster Tolchard said, 'I think I could have caught a cold.'

'I do apologize, I've got nothing but Russian brandy.' Field extended a hip flask. 'The Russians are as useless at brandy as they are at space probes. What wouldn't I give for just a gulp of the old Hennessey? Still buggers can't be choosers, as dear old Guy Burgess used to say. What's the news of Patsy Hendren these days?'

'I think I may be catching pneumonia,' Buster Tolchard said, sucking at the fierce liquid.

'I hope you're not going to die on me.' The master traitor smiled frostily. 'It's so seldom I get a chance to talk to people from home. I'm surrounded by peasants here, people who've never heard of Dimple Haig or Michael Brearley. By the way I hear Laurence Olivier and Vivien Leigh have split up.'

'There's no bath in my hotel, not even a shower,' Tolchard thought aloud. 'I don't know how I'm going to shake these shivers off.'

'Sievers, M. W.,' the KGB General brightened, 'Australian all-rounder in the '36–'37 season if I remember all right. Got Hammond twice at Melbourne and Walter Robins for a duck at Brisbane. But that was nothing to write home about. Seen anything of Maurice Leyland recently?'

'I will be dead if I don't get out of these clothes,' Buster answered.

'Don't worry, as soon as we get ashore I'll get Vasili to run you a hot bath.'

'No thank you!'

'Never mind, I'm sure we'll think of something. But tell me about Eddie Paynter. You know it was criminal not to send him to Australia with Gubby Allen's team. And yet they found a berth for old Arthur Fagg! It cost them the series that omission you know – that and a few other oversights.'

Ask him what he remembers of the English cricket season of 1937. These were Tolchard's orders. This was the question he had travelled miles, at no negligible risk, to ask. Now he was in the arch-traitor's presence the question seemed almost superfluous. Tristan Field apparently inhabited a time capsule almost exclusively peopled by cricketers and show-business personalities of the season of 1937 or thereabouts. Orders were orders, however, and in any case, escape was blocked by the threat of Vasili's hot bath.

'What do you remember of the English cricket season of 1937?' Buster dutifully enquired.

The sun was shining blisteringly on the Gorky Park lake-waters; but the darkest of shadows was moving across Tristan Field's face.

'I remember a certain amount of youthful achievement,' he answered. 'I also remember discovering that English officialdom is bigoted, purblind, corrupt, venal and altogether *vile*!'

Poking with the ferrule of his umbrella at the pavement outside Green Park underground station, James Ball had given Tolchard a further briefing on his Moscow mission for which he was shortly to depart by the Piccadilly Line to Heathrow and a special discount Intourist Aeroflot flight. In fact, time had been so short and Ball had been so perversely long-winded that Buster had had to hump his luggage onto the Heathrow tube train before Ball had made his directions altogether clear. On one point, however, his mentor had been specific. If Field reacted to the question, he was to be drawn out and encouraged into confidences.

'You made 130 runs for the Gentlemen that year, didn't you?' Buster said, trying to fight the cold in his bones and the hate in his heart for the traitor at the oars.

'151 runs if you don't mind!' Field snapped. 'I would have thought Bally would have made sure you got your figures right!'

'And 250 against Glamorgan the following week.'

'263 please!' the KGB General snarled. 'Where on earth were you brought up? – I can't honestly believe it was Harrow!' he added with a savage glance at Tolchard's dripping tie.

'I know a lot of people thought you should have been picked for England,' Tolchard continued with as much sympathy as he could pressure into his voice. He was thinking of James Ball's ferrule probing the Green Park pavement. 'Try and forget the laughing-stock he's made us throughout the security world and all our agents he's had shot,' his mentor's measured tones played back in his mind. 'Try and imagine how it must feel to be passed over for England – and sympathize.'

'Of course I should have been picked for England my dear damp friend,' Field answered with a withering smile. He stopped pulling at the oars. For a few anxious seconds Tolchard thought he was going to strike him with one of them. It turned out he was only shipping them. Now they were floating. Two men on a lake which might have been an ocean.

'Of course I should have been picked for England,' Field repeated, 'that must have been clear to the dimmest peasant in the land. What must have been equally obvious, at least to anyone with the crudest knowledge of the game, is that I should have been the England skipper!'

'Really? I mean what bad luck!' Above all be sympathetic Ball had urged.

'Well look at alternatives!' Field waved his bleached artistic hands. 'R. E. S. Wyatt? Far too accident-prone. Gubby Allen? A good trier, a reasonable speedster but increasingly out of practice because of his business dealings. R. W. V. Robins? "A useful all-rounder" as they used to say. Short of centuries as a batsman and short of a length as a bowler. The old duffers in the Long Room liked to describe him as a "captain of spirit", meaning that Walter wasn't too strong on brains. Still Walter Robins got the vote, at least until they gave up trying to find a gentleman and tossed the mantle at poor old Hammond – a marvellous figure of a man, of course, but absolutely no Albert Einstein! No, if you look at England's captaincy selections before the war you can discern only one consistent thread of reason – a determination at all costs to avoid the obvious choice of T. G. K. Yellowfield. I don't suppose you have a Players Navy Cut cigarette on you by any chance? Sorry, I forgot you're too wet for it to be smokable even if you had one.'

Field clawed a pack of Russian cigarettes from his Free Forrester blazer and placed a cardboard filter in his mouth with an expression of wry distaste.

'You see I had the brains as well as the strokes,' he continued. 'Eton versus Harrow 1932 – the rowdies from the Hill sent tumbling to defeat by an innings and sixteen runs. Did it ever occur to those foolish, wicked old men to consider who was the master strategist behind that astonishing victory? If they did they chose to ignore the evidence! Oxford versus the Australians, 1934. Chalk retires to the pavy for half an hour with a gammy leg and Yellowfield takes temporary command. In that short space of time we get three of the buggers out for 35 runs. Did those lobster-brained old dugouts ever pause to ponder the reason why? You can jolly well bet they didn't!

'You see I was the only man in England who knew how to get Bradman out,' the KGB general revealed with a strange gleam in his cloud-grey eyes. 'The theory was that he didn't like pace. That was rubbish. He devoured it with both hands like the badly brought up little colonial he was. No, the only way to get Bradman was nagging medium pace and a deep set field – slow his run rate, shame the little colonial into making a fatal mistake. I had the measure of Macabe and Headley too for that matter. I don't think it's any exaggeration to say I could have won back the Ashes in 1938 and routed the West Indies in '39. I will go further: if I had still been in the game I would have held the green-caps to a draw in '46 – '47, even with that sorry lot they sent out with poor old Walter Hammond. Under me we would have wiped the floor with Bradman's 1948 Australians. Without wishing to flatter myself, I think I would have safely seen off those two over-rated blackamoors, friends Ramadhin and Valentine, in that catastrophic West Indian summer. Too old to captain England in 1950, do I hear you murmur? My dear fellow I was but a year the senior of N. W. D. Yardley – the not-so-nimble blue-eyed boy of the old brigade who steered England to yet another Dunkirk in that shaming series. I tell you, my dear young water rat, I could have re-written the history of English cricket in those locust years, and incidentally totally upset, in the process, my own theory that there is an odd relationship between England's performance on the cricket field and the state of the nation.'

If Tolchard had been privileged to attend a certain lecture at KGB headquarters earlier in the year he would have been struck by the similarity of this concept to that expressed, at somewhat greater length, by one Professor Yakov of the Statistical Department.

The lake was ringed with bunting and also loud speakers. When not required for official announcements they broadcast musical selections by the disc-jockey charwoman in the boat-house. At this moment she was playing Tchaikovsky's 'Nut-cracker Suite' for at least the fourth time.

'I don't suppose you brought any decent records with you?' Field wondered. 'Anything new by Ted Heath or Geraldo. They have absolutely no sense of rhythm in this blessed country, as you can hear for yourself. Not even a few Victor Silvester fox-trots? Pity. Never mind. They'd have probably confiscated them even if you had tried to bring them in. Thank God for Evelyn Lilliwhite at the "Oval", the old sweetie does keep me supplied with the odd Jack Buchanan through the diplomatic bag.'

'You were talking about the England captaincy,' Tolchard reminded him from a haze of steam. The blistering sun was at last getting to work on wet clothes, sucking moisture from the sodden material with visible effect.

'It stuck out a mile that it should have been mine. So of course they had to resort to dirty tricks, as the CIA would say. Oh yes, I'm well aware of that disgraceful smear that was spread about me – that malignant insinuation that was spread about the County circuit that I didn't fancy the fast stuff. I tell you they were lying through their decaying teeth!' Field leaned forward to hiss at the visiting Englishman. 'Maybe the luck didn't run for me at Trent Bridge that summer, but I demolished Ken Farnes in Colchester week. No, the truth of the matter was altogether seamier – it was rooted in the moral hypocrisy and obscene sexual envy of that flatulent gang of old humbugs.

'You see I cut a bit of a dash with the ladies in those days, or you might say the girls. It had not escaped the notice of the old haddocks that I was currently escorting a luscious young girl from Rodean. The fact that she was still attending Rodean was immaterial as far as I was concerend. In everything that mattered she was a fully developed woman. But the dirty old humbugs of Lord's chose to smell moral turpitude in our frankly rather beautiful liaison – Yellowfield was playing with jail-bait in their prurient view. Believe me, if you'd known Jan as I knew Jan you'd have appreciated there was nothing more that particular school girl needed to learn. Jan Bailey, what a peach!' Field mused dreamily. 'Never could understand why she decided to marry that dreary James Ball.'

Now Buster Tolchard knew that he was in the presence of total evil – evil that corrupted whatever it touched. He realized that Tristan Field's treachery did not end with all the atom secrets he had betrayed. He had planted his corrosive sting at the heart of his country's moral life. Tolchard was not a man of boundless imagination; but he could picture how Jan Ball might have been before Yellowfield touched her with his poison. A pretty, smiling schoolgirl with features as fresh as a Lord's sky. A girl to whom any decent man might have respectfully touched his hat. If he had entertained any tender thoughts about her they would have been conditioned by the wholesome proviso that no romantic approach could be contemplated until her school blazer had long been packed away. Then the painted, raddled face of Jan Ball as she was today presented itself for his mind's inspection. Surely it was Yellowfield's poisonous kiss that had begun the process of shocking decay. The woman who constantly brought shame to James Ball and even, it could be argued, to England itself was the corrupted child of the supreme traitor. Tolchard's knuckles gleamed white on the rowing boat's gunwales.

'So there it was.' Field sank his teeth into another cardboard cigarette filter. 'No place for T. G. K. Yellowfield and certainly no captaincy. Nothing. Not a sausage! There was some talk of me being in line to captain the MCC tour of Holland and Denmark that autumn, but they even denied me that. People call me a traitor you know; but I would point the finger straight at the Committee Room of Lord's. To deny England the ability and the brains of T. G. K. Yellowfield – that was the supreme treason!'

'Just because you had a grudge against the Selectors you sold your country to its deadliest enemy,' Buster growled, intensifying his grip on the gunwales. A fire-ball of anger was welling up inside him, speeding the drying process which the sun had begun.

Tristan Field's face split into an exultant smile.

'Well you have to admit that England has certainly lived to rue my omission. They haven't won a winter tour in years. One disaster after another. And judging from what I read in *The Times* it's an absolutely calamitous summer!'

Something in Tolchard snapped. He could no longer keep his fists locked to the gunwales. The creature – he could not call him a man – was sitting there laughing, luxuriating in all the evil he had wrought in the Eden that had once been England. He had to hit him. Thrust honest knuckle bone into that powdery, purple-veined face. Smash the bulbous arrogance in that beak of a nose. He clambered up perhaps a little too quickly. He was on his feet, but his legs were already committed to a battle for balance.

'Sit down, you're rocking the boat,' Field ordered him with a serpentine sneer. 'My God,' he added, 'you're as clumsy as an England three-quarter!'

The taunt tore away the last restraints of caution. Tolchard advanced his left foot as if into a punishing on drive and swung with his right fist. The rowing boat dipped hard to port and then lurched to starboard. Now Field was gripping the gunwales. Buster could read the fear in his face – fear crossed with a savage desire for self-preservation. He threw forward his right foot with the double motive of regaining his balance and closing the distance between himself and his target. His foot impacted with the boat floor when it was already dangerously tipped to starboard. He stamped wildly with his left foot to counter-balance and found himself treading water. And then the lake's muddy liquid was closing over his head again.

When he surfaced he saw that the rowing boat was still afloat. The figure in a panama and Free Forester blazer was rowing strenuously in the opposite direction.

'Give my regards to James and Jan,' Field briefly waved, 'and do remember me to Bill Edrich.'

24
A GAME OF CROQUET

PRIVATE & CONFIDENTIAL

Sir Ambrose Darcy, MBE
Newbury Castle
Lambourn
Berks

Dear Sir Ambrose,

As you may have heard, Umpire Reginald Peat is due to be released from Strangeways Prison, Manchester, this morning by Royal pardon. I would be extremely grateful if, even at this late stage, you could arrange for Peat to stand at the Nottingham Test on Thursday. I can assure you that he is now a completely reformed character and anxious to make amends for his previous lapse.

I feel we all have a responsibility towards the rehabilitation of convicted offenders, especially those of us who are in no position to cast the first stone. For instance, I have on my desk at this moment a number of documents dealing with your Cayman Islands re-insurance operations which, if released to the Fraud Squad, would be sufficient to ensure you an even more severe sentence than that endured by the unfortunate Peat. I am sure I do not need to draw your attention to the further penalties which would almost certainly be levelled, namely liquidation of your partnerships and the forfeit of your Name by Ian Hay Davison, otherwise known as 'Mr Clean'.

Please don't trouble to reply. An announcement in the newspapers to the effect that Peat will be substituting for Umpire Constant who is indisposed will be quite satisfactory.

Yours sincerely,
James Ball

Ball grimly sealed the letter and affixed a commemorative stamp. It had not been an easy letter to write. The nearby wastepaper basket was stuffed with earlier drafts. He was only too painfully aware that what he had written was not cricket. Yet he reminded himself that the stakes had become too high for decency and sportsmanship. The paradox of the situation twisted his lips into a mordant smile – in order to save English cricket it had become necessary to take off the gloves and play baseball.

'I'm just popping out for a moment,' he called upstairs, although Jan, as it happened, was not at home. Had she been in she would have recognized the strangled appeal for sympathy contained in these few words. In the Ball family's book 'popping out for a moment' meant he was departing on another confrontation with danger. This morning, Ball knew that he was embarked for perhaps the most formidable confrontation he had ever faced.

It could, of course, still be avoided, James told himself as he cruised in a hired Rover down the Kingston by-pass. It could be argued that it was not strictly necessary to accept Hector Bootle's invitation to Saturday lunch at Esher. The battle could, arguably, still be waged by remote control. But in the honesty of his heart, Ball recognized that there was no real alternative to meeting the enemy face-to-face. To avoid the encounter would have signalled fear – to the enemy and to his own soul. No frightened king or captain ever won a battle or a Test Match, Ball dourly reminded himself as he left the Guildford road and headed into the pines of Esher's opulent outskirts.

Hector himself opened the mock-Tudor door of his mansion.

Ball noted he was wearing his sleeves rolled and a cook's apron.

'James how splendid to see you. You catch me in the act of peeling the potatoes. But come in do. She's longing to meet you. Incidentally have you heard about my spot of luck? They've extended my leave indefinitely. We're living in a leisured paradise here. Of course Melanie has to commute to her studies. Bless her clever little socks, she's working on a thesis about English Social History; but she doesn't forget the old man for too long. By the way I hope you play croquet. She's an absolute corker at croquet.'

Ball followed his host into a massive drawing room, to judge by its furnishings and appointments his wife would have called it 'the lounge'. A pair of Gothic French windows were open on a blazing green lawn. Through them a girl was slowly sauntering. There could be no question as to the voluptuousness of her figure. She was very nearly naked. The briefest of kerchiefs, briefer by far than he had been led to expect, incompletely covered a pair of fabulous breasts. At her waist, far below her exposed navel, she wore a pair of white cricket shorts, short enough for a boy in his first term at prep school. They were unnecessarily supported by an old Wellingtonian tie – Ball's old school.

As she neared him he noticed her scent – not a musky rich perfume such as Jan was wont to drench herself with. This scent was light as champagne or sunshine on blue southern waters, as subtly intoxicating as a cool glass of lemonade laced with vodka.

'Do not trouble please to introduce us, Hector,' she drawled. 'I feel already I know Mr Ball so well.'

She extended a golden arm in a manner which seemed to invite a kiss on the hand. Ball pointedly shook it.

'I too have heard much about you,' he smiled courteously, 'though I confess to being less certain about your name.'

'I told you this is Melanie, the one and only,' Bootle called from the cocktail cabinet. 'You're getting bloody forgetful in your old age, James.'

'Melanie, of course. I don't know how I got it into my head

the name was Stephanie.'

Their eyes were already in contact, deliberately in James's case, since he had dared not lower them. He waited for a reaction in these azure eyes which Hector had accurately described as devastating. Not an eyelash quivered.

'Are you really so forgetful?' she smiled. 'Hector tells me you are an excellent counter-spy. That I think takes a good memory, Mr Bally.'

'The name is Ball as a matter of fact,' he politely corrected her.

'But am I not right in saying it is "Bally" to your intimate friends? I would wish to be your intimate friend, James.'

'Good health everybody,' Hector beamed over a tray of gin and tonic jugs. 'Well what do you think of her, James? That's right you're lost for words. I dare say even Keats would have had his work cut out doing justice to Melanie. But look, we don't want to stay indoors on a day like this. Let's take our drinks onto the patio.'

'The potatoes, darling,' the girl who called herself Melanie purred.

'Oh yes, I was peeling the potatoes, wasn't I.'

'And seeing to the joint,' she prompted.

'Of course. Tell you what, why don't you play a game of croquet with Melanie while I'm doing the potatoes and seeing to the joint? I warn you she's an absolute marvel with a mallet.' Bootle's burly frame exited for the kitchen.

Ball swallowed hard at his gin and tonic and followed the girl out into the extravagant sunshine.

She turned to him with a sly smile. 'You are looking hot and bothered Mr Bally. You must take off your pin-stripe jacket and remove this tie.' He felt a light tug on his Civil Servant Association tie, and knew that it was directed at his heart-strings.

'I'm quite comfortable as I am, thank you,' he answered with a hint of asperity.

She handed him a mallet from Fortnum & Mason. It was almost brand new. White wood. Gleaming copper rings. He estimated Hector would have had to fork out nearly £500 for this new croquet set and it was likely to have been merely one of the woman's whims.

'I know you are a gentleman, Mr Bally. So you will insist on saying "ladies first". Very well I will go first; but I am sure I am not so good at the croquet as you.'

She stepped in front of him and leaned over her mallet to take aim. Even for a man of Ball's years she presented an agonizingly provocative spectacle. The motion of bending had stretched the boy's cricket shorts dangerously tight across her superbly shaped bum. As he coughed with muzzled desire, Ball could not help but marvel at the arrogant calculation behind the effect. He suspected now that the white shorts had been deliberately chosen to stir memories among old public school boys of illicit desires on long ago cricket boundaries. In other words this formidable creature was flaunting more than her own outrageous female sexuality. She was unlocking a door which every normal man had slammed forever on leaving school – the shaming appeal of a younger boy in whites. The old school tie was, of course, an essential accessory to the ambiguous effect. For L. M. S. Partridge she had no doubt worn an Old Harrovian tie, for Hector Bootle the tie of his old school, if he had had one. The realization that his instincts were being deliberately manipulated enabled Ball to fight off an impulse to step forward and put his hand on the creature's posterior.

Meanwhile the girl who called herself Melanie had taken scrupulously careful aim. Prompted by a resonant clip, the croquet ball sped from the coloured post towards the first hoop. It seemed on the point of bypassing its goal on account of the angle; but the girl had imparted latent spin. In the mouth of the hoop the ball abruptly changed direction and sped through the prongs, clean as a Dusty Hare penalty.

'No Mr Bally. You are not, please, holding your mallet the right way. As perhaps sometimes you do not handle your investigations in the right way. Let me show you how you would do well to trust Melanie.'

Now he was imprisoned by a pair of golden arms. He felt cool subtle hands brush his trousers teasingly before they locked on his hands.

'There, you see that is so much an easier grip,' her whispered words caressed his ear. 'Now you are holding your mallet firmly, as I know you could hold a woman very firmly. No do not frown like that, Mr Bally. You must not be suspicious of peoples who are only wishing to help you, only wanting to be your intimate friend.'

'I've been playing this game a few years, you know.' James elbowed himself out of the girl's intoxicating embrace and tried to steady himself for a perfect shot. It wasn't a bad shot in the circumstances. The ball sped across the polished Kentucky blue grass on a direct line for the hoop. But it was imbued with no latent spin. It struck the side of the hoop and came to a stop at an impossibly disadvantageous angle.

'That is a pity. You did not listen to your good counsellor. Now you must pay a bad forfeit.' She picked up her bright yellow ball and placed it against his stalled red one. 'See I have gone through the hoop and you have failed. Now I am entitled to give you a hard knock.' On a short handle she clipped down on her ball and sent his bounding over the lawn to crash into a laurel thicket.

It was a rule of the game he had never before encountered, but at least it was cooler among the laurels. The posture was, of course, far from dignified – groping on hands and knees for a lost croquet ball which had been dispatched with the power of a Graham Gooch off-drive. Yet here was cover from the blazing sun and the scorching sexuality of his antagonist.

'Mr Ball I have found your ball.'

He looked up and saw a foreign colour among the shadowed leaves – a mane of auburn hair as lustrous as a Riviera or even a Dorking sunset. Then he saw a gleaming bronzed arm reach out of the undergrowth to offer him a red ball. He looked closer. He saw an apparition of temptation which no longer carried any overtones of schoolboy lust. He saw a woman almost as naked as Eve and at least as desirable in her flagrant femininity. A vision of primeval desire which could make a proffered croquet ball almost as irresistible as the first apple.

Ball's glasses were misting over. But he did not fail to notice the serpentine way in which she licked the red croquet ball before she placed it nearly within his grasp.

'You see I am your good playmate,' a silken soft voice seemed to boom in his ears. 'You lose your balls. I find them. Can your leaders offer you so much?'

Adam may have lingered. James snatched the ball from its teasing presenter and strode back onto the croquet lawn.

'Let's try our luck on the next hoop,' he panted.

As she indicated, it was her privilege to go first. A click of a mallet on a yellow ball and she was through the second hoop like a conversion by Campbell of Ireland.

James took a grip low down the mallet's handle, tried to think himself into the position of a potential Ryder Cup winner on the eighteenth hole of St Andrew's, tried to dream his cumbersome Fortnum & Mason mallet into a top professional's putter. His red ball sped truly along the path already charted by the girl who called herself Melanie and impacted with her bright yellow ball.

'Oh Mr Bally, that was not so clever. You have collided with my ball. This is meaning I have two chances to hit you out of play.'

Away like an on drive by Gordon Greenidge bounded the red ball, deep into a forest of spent rhododendrons. He was back in a jungle of indignity, looking for a red ball, fighting fatigue, desire and surrender and the possibility of a fatal cardiac.

'Look, Mr Bally you are not so good-sighted,' he could hear a velvet siren's voice overhead. 'You think your friends are that old woman Prime Minister and that so immature and ridiculous young fascist you call Buster Tolchard. But see, I am the intimate friend who finds your balls. Why do you wish to resist me?'

He tried to scramble out of the seductive voice's earshot: but discovered his head was restrained by a clamped pair of sun-fed thighs.

'Perhaps, Mr Bally, you would prefer to play cricket,' the

imprisoning temptress' voice crooned. 'Perhaps you would rather play at bowling the Nawab of Pataudi or tricking Viv Richards with your wrong one. I will be your helper and accomplice. Listen to your good counsellor, Mr Bally. I know more about cricket even than your Mr Benny Green. I can make your very wildest fantasies come true. Or perhaps,' an electric hand ruffled his remaining grey hairs, 'you do not want to play at croquet or cricket. You want only to play with your Melanie. That would be so understandable. Look up at me, Mr Bally. Does a man need any other sport when he has his Melanie?'

'I think I hear the luncheon bell.' James said, grasping as if at straws, although it was true that Hector Bootle in his apron had emerged onto the patio and was pounding a copper gong.

'Hector will wait, as long as I am telling him. He eats out of my hand.'

James Ball fought back with the resolution of a John Bull. 'I'm possibly a little old fashioned, but I don't like my roast beef overdone.'

'And these lips, Mr Bally. Are these lips, as you say, overdone?'

Lips as red as a bed of Surrey roses, as moist and as inviting as a rare porterhouse steak, less than an inch from his mouth.

'I'm not L. M. S. Partridge you know,' he stammered out defiantly. 'I'm not so easily twisted round your little finger.'

'Now you are being a wicked man,' she chided as she wound his supine body round her waist. 'You are talking of other womans when you know there is only one Melanie. You have only to trust her, to take her in your still strong arms and you will forget all about Lionel Partridge and his so boring cricket. You will think no more of the cold wars and your not so warming Mrs Jan. You will think only of the warmth of this mouth.'

'Close your eyes and think of England!' Words of advice spoken long ago in a housemaster's study rushed, as if by time telegraph, into his mind. He had smirked at this platitudinous homily then. Seven simple words to keep at one's fingertips, his old housemaster had urged him, in the event of finding oneself in the path of Temptation. Now he thanked the blue Surrey heavens that these seven simple words had been miraculously rescued from time's wastepaper basket.

He closed his eyes. He thought of England. He thought of callow, pimply faces looking out sheepishly from under the peaks of brand new, ill-fitting caps. He thought of the names – Noads, Pew, Blisset, Carstairs and Duck and he winced at the shame these hapless nonentities had brought upon the three Leopards of England. Then, as if struck by a douche of cold water, he was reminded that the fiend responsible for his country's humiliation was less then an inch away.

'I'm sorry, but I really am rather peckish,' Ball spring-jacked to his feet, wiping dead rhododendron blooms from his trousers with deliberate fastidiousness. The moment of supreme danger had come. Thanks to a long dead public school housemaster it had passed.

25
THE LAW'S DELAY

'The good news,' Brian Johnston announced, 'is that we've got a wonderful day for cricket. I don't know about you Freddie, but I don't think I've ever seen such a beautiful day at Nottingham. I don't know about you but I would think that old George Gunn would have looked to have two hundred runs on the board on this strip before lunchtime. But unfortunately we don't have George Gunn in the England team today. In fact, we don't seem to have many familiar names. That's something I know Freddie and Trevor will want to talk about because, of course, there have been just a few Press comments about the selection of this England team.'

'If you ask me it's a downright disgrace.'

'But in the meantime, Freddie, the news is that England have won the toss and are batting. Now normally that would be jolly good news for England, but with this present England team there could be just a few little doubts about their ability to cope with any early-morning life there could be in this wicket.'

'They just don't have the application.'

'Well, of course, Trevor, there is just that little niggle of worry; but in the meantime we've got umpire Reg Peat making a second wicket inspection. In fact, he's not looking at the wicket, he's looking at the light – holding his light meter up against the sun just to make sure that conditions are right for play. Incidentally, it's a little bit of a surprise to see that Umpire Peat is standing in this Test after that small spot of bother we had in the First Test at Old Trafford. But that's obviously all behind him now and we're looking forward to a jolly exciting day's cricket.'

'If this bunch can survive until lunchtime we could have a full day's play Brian.'

'I'm sorry I've got to interrupt you there, Freddie, because the Australians are on the field and here comes England's opening pair – Ken Noads and Benny Blisset.'

'They're about worth a pair – the two of them.'

'And it's my turn to hand you over to Tony Lewis.'

'Ken Noads, a little ferret of a man, takes guard and carves out his block-hole like a small mole going to ground,' England's former Welsh captain lyricized. 'Now he's looking around the field with a kind of toad-like apprehension. There's no doubt he's only too well aware of the enormous responsibility resting on his young, sloping shoulders.'

'He's taking middle stump. In his position I would have certainly been inclined to take middle and leg.'

'Well that's quite true Trevor, because Geoff Lawson who is measuring out his run now is a bowler who can produce a phenomenal amount of in-swing – in-swing combined with impressive speed. And here comes the first ball of the Fourth Test. And Noads shoulders arms to that one to let it go through to the wicketkeeper. But there's that phenomenal in-swing I've been talking about. The ball has uprooted his leg stump.'

'Test match statistics go back a long way,' Henry Blofeld cut in, 'but I'm wondering if anyone can tell us if England has ever made a worse start to a Test first innings in this country.'

Brian Johnston recalled himself to the microphone. 'But here's an interesting development, Henry. Umpire Peat is looking at the light. Now as far as I can see there's not much wrong with the light. It's a cloudless summer day.'

'There is a cloud, Brian, perhaps no smaller than a man's hand just shading the sun,' Trevor Bailey pointed out.

'And that's clearly what's worrying Umpire Peat,' Tony Lewis said. 'That little wisp of cloud just masking the lower half of the sun there.'

'He's consulting with Umpire Dicky Bird now.'

'Now Umpire Bird is holding his meter up to the sun; but he's definitely staying put. I agree with you Brian, it's the best day we ever had for a Test at Trent Bridge.'

'Yes, Umpire Bird is waving play on; but Umpire Peat is still unhappy. He's pointing at his light meter out there, and presumably it's showing insufficient lumens. And of course one must assume that with that little scientific instrument which all Test umpires carry nowadays he's in a better position to judge conditions out there than we are in here.'

'Best light I ever saw at Trent Bridge – least since my first season. And that's going back to 1949.'

'Now Umpire Peat is pointing up at the sun and it's true, I suppose, that that little wisp of cloud is covering just a fraction more of its surface. I imagine that what's in Umpire Peat's mind is that the Australians have some pretty fast bowlers in their attack, and he doesn't want to risk broken limbs in suspect light. And of course when you've got one umpire who's unhappy with conditions you've got a problem – perhaps it's a fault of the current legislation – because you haven't got a casting vote. In any case the problem has been resolved because they're coming off – coming off for bad light, even though Umpire Bird is still out there pointing at the sun and trying to wave play on. And now Umpire Peat is calling for the covers. This could mean quite a long delay.'

'Well thank you, Tony, and of course we will be continuing our commentary just as soon as play is resumed. But in the meantime,' broadcasting's most assured professional chatted on, 'we've got bags of listeners' letters to answer. But first I'd like to send a very hearty message of thanks to Mrs Isobel Freud of Reigate for the absolutely super chocolate cake she's baked us. It will go down jolly well with the claret, won't it Trevor?'

Back in St. John's Wood, James Ball gestured towards a television screen picturing a cricket pitch covered with tarpaulin with one member of the Nottinghamshire ground staff standing sentinel in his shirt sleeves.

'Don't look so despondent,' he turned to Buster Tolchard, only recently returned from Moscow, with a nearly mischievous grin, 'there's still a chance we can make a draw of it.'

' . . . but it's time now to greet new listeners with the news that England here on the first day at Trent Bridge are nought for one wicket and that play has been interrupted by bad light. That's the bad news. The good news is that the players are taking an early lunch and that we're hoping for a resumption around 2.30. Meanwhile the sun is blistering down on this lovely batting strip. So we'll be hoping that when play resumes, if it does resume, that England's batsmen will be able to make the most of it. Now I'm handing you over to Trevor Bailey for his impressions of the morning's play. . . . '

' . . . and here at last come the umpires and it looks as if we're finally going to get a resumption of play on this first afternoon of the Fourth Test at Trent Bridge, although Umpire Peat is looking a little dubiously at the ribbon of cloud away to our left over the Trent Bridge hotel.'

'That's not a cloud, Brian, it's a string of washing,' Freddie Trueman said.

'All the same Umpire Peat is giving it a pretty dirty look. But now here come the players, no doubt keen to get their muscles moving after their enforced rest. Certainly everyone must be hoping we're going to see some cricket before the tea interval. But here is young Miles Watford of Somerset taking guard and, of course, because the players went off for light immediately after the fall of the first wicket he's yet to receive a ball. Trevor a brief profile of Miles Watford.

'It better be brief at that,' Freddie Trueman commented, 'because from the look of 'is stance 'es not going to be out there long.'

'To be honest Brian, Miles Watford is a bit of a dark horse to me. He's certainly a newcomer to Test cricket. In fact I'm not sure if he's yet been awarded his county cap. Can anyone tell me if he's been awarded his county cap?'

'I'm sorry to interrupt you there, Trevor, but Miles Watford has been hit on the pad and an enormous appeal has gone up. A quite deafening appeal. Every man in the field is on his toes shouting at Umpire Peat. But he's taking his time. He's not going to be intimidated. But I think his finger is going up. No, he's pointing at the sun. I think he's indicating that he's been unsighted by the sun. It looks as if Miles Watford can breathe again. Now Umpire Peat is walking over to Umpire Bird, pointing at his eyes and then at the sun. I think he's telling him the sun which is going down a little now is shining directly into his face and making decisions difficult. Yes that must be the reason because Umpire Peat is coming off.'

'Could be a call of nature, Brian.'

'Well no because now everyone is coming off, a little reluctantly perhaps, but of course you can't play a Test match with an umpire off the field, though from the way he's tearing his hair it looks as if Umpire Bird is quite prepared to play on. And now there's a loudspeaker announcement. Can you hear what they're saying, Freddie? Yes, well there we are. No play until the sun has gone down sufficiently not to get in Umpire Peat's eyes. Meanwhile, we understand, the players will be taking an early tea.'

'So we'd like to welcome listeners to Trent Bridge for the second day's play of the Fourth Test Match. There's been a spot of rain on the wicket earlier this morning, and Umpire Peat is out there examining it now.'

'He's going to need a bloody magnifying glass.'

'Well it's certainly turned out a gorgeous day, Freddie, and I'm sure all of us will be hoping for a prompt start and keeping our fingers crossed that we're going to see England really knuckle down and improve on their overnight score of 19 for 3 which conceivably could be even worse if we'd had a full day's play yesterday. Would you agree with me there, Trevor?'

'There is, I'm afraid, a disturbing lack of application about this present England side – and, I might add, of basic cricketing skills. . . .'

'I'm sorry I've got to interrupt you there, Trevor, we're getting a loudspeaker announcement. What are they saying, Henry? I can't hear because Henry is munching a fruit drop. Really? Well that is a little bit of a disappointment, because quite honestly we haven't got any more readers' letters left. Apparently, Umpire Peat is not satisfied the pitch is fit for play. It seems that early morning drop of rain has slipped through the covers and caused a damp spot on the wicket. Well there you have it from the horse's mouth, as it were. It's caused a little bit of good natured banter from the crowd; but we are promised a second pitch inspection at 12.30 . . . .'

On the television screen, the dome-like head of veteran commentator Peter West eclipsed the Trent Bridge sunlight. 'On the face of it we have the ideal conditions for play here in Nottingham,' he spoke tersely to camera, 'which only goes to show you never can tell in this game of cricket.'

'That foul, slimy little crook Reg Peat's behind this!' Buster Tolchard had sprung out of his chair and was shaking his fist at the screen. 'Whoever let that grisly criminal out of Strangeways ought to be put up against a wall and shot!'

'Easy now Buster,' James Ball called soothingly from his armchair. 'You know as well as I do we cannot afford to lose this Test.'

'Yes, but dash it – this fellow Peat!'

'Look again at the England batting order – their batting order, Buster – and ask yourself who else could possibly save this Test for us?'

'Good God!' Tolchard's aggressive honest face turned to his host. His bushy eyebrows formed into a troubled question-mark. 'You mean to say, I should say Sir, you had something to do with getting that poisonous individual out of jail, fixing it so he could stand in this Test?'

'We are playing at Clausewitz, not cricket, Buster, and time is not on our side. While we are waiting for the 12.30 pitch inspection, I want you to tell me again exactly what you remember of your conversation with General Tristan Field, formerly Yellowfield. I appreciate it was a depressing not to say dampening experience; but more than a series depends on your memory, Buster,' James said without a hint of a smile.

26

AN INVITATION FROM THE MCC

'Are you putting a pistol to my head?' asked the Secretary of the MCC.

He had been working late over letters in the Committee Room. The empty field of play in front of him was, as Francis Thompson might have said, full of shades. All his colleagues were at Trent Bridge for the Test Match. He was alone in Lord's with the ghosts of a thousand legendary fixtures – or so he had thought until the two intruders had stealthily entered the Committee Room and he had seen from the purposeful expression on their faces that they were not phantoms.

'There's no question of putting a pistol to your head, Secretary,' James Ball blandly reassured him, 'although, as it happens, Buster here carries a Walther P38 for self protection. We are merely making an urgent request.'

'It's going to be rather difficult to accommodate you.' The Secretary slightly relaxed. 'You see we've already offered the captaincy of the Holland and Denmark tour to Lord Eastbourne's son. Between you and me he is a very substantial contributor to club and ground charities.'

'Secretary, without putting a pistol to your head, I have to tell you that unless you are able to meet us in this matter, a bill for the privatization of Lord's will be introduced into Parliament in the next session. That is perhaps a measure of the backing we have for our request,' Ball replied grimly.

'He's such an unsuitable person to captain an MCC party abroad,' the Secretary complained, 'especially since I gather he sets no kind of example in facing the fast stuff.'

'If you would be good enough to write as I dictate, Secretary, on this sheet of MCC notepaper,' Ball insisted, 'I have no doubt that the Prime Minister will wish to make a special exception in your case to her wide-ranging privatization plans.'

'I suppose I have no alternative. What does the odious little turd call himself nowadays?'

'Address him as T. G. K. Yellowfield Esq., c.o. General Tristan Field, KGB Central Headquarters, Moscow, USSR. May I suggest how you should continue?'

'I suppose so; but don't go too fast,' said the Secretary grumpily.

This was the text of the letter that emerged.

Dear Yellowfield,

I wonder if you would be available from 29 August to 15 September to captain the forthcoming MCC tour of Holland and Denmark. There will be two unofficial 'Tests' at the Hague and at Copenhagen, and the Committee are confident that your special blend of experience and tactical ability will be just what is required to ensure there are no dramatic upsets for English cricket in a part of the world where we are still expected to excel.

The Committee have taken cognizance of the fact that your name was passed over with insufficient consideration for the corresponding tour in 1937. They trust you will see this appointment as a sincere endeavour to rectify matters. In parenthesis I might add that while the Committee of the MCC is no longer empowered to make appointments to the England captaincy, there can be no doubt that the Holland-Denmark tour has often proved a successful testing ground for future England leaders.

As you will see from the enclosed fixture card, the tour will commence with a one-day match against Spandau Prison

(British Army contingent) in West Berlin. This could be a convenient point at which to join your party.

I look forward to your reply and trust I will be able to inform my Committee of your acceptance.

I am yours very sincerely,

J. Spriggs
Secretary, MCC

PS With your acceptance, perhaps you would also kindly confirm that you will be countenancing no further attempts to undermine the English game, and that any agents that may have been engaged to this purpose have been withdrawn at your express orders.

'It will have to wait till tomorrow,' the Secretary said, as he slid the letter into his desk drawer. 'I'm completely out of stamps.'

'No stamp will be necessary.' Ball slid the letter out of the drawer and folded it into an appropriate MCC envelope. 'This letter will travel to Moscow tonight by diplomatic bag.'

27
COURT REPORT

'Have I anything to say in my defence before I am sentenced?' Umpire Reg Peat glowered out of his box up at the podium of justice. 'I should blooming well think I have! All right, squire, I may have made one small error. I gave your Abraham Udu out lbw. But don't forget, your honour, a Taffy is always plumb in front, even if there's maybe a few inches either way in it, or even if your greasy little Welsh bastard happens to be as black as a Cardiff coal tip. I'm not prejudiced, Sir. I merely draw the line at wogs of all colours as start at Newport.'

'Will the prisoner be good enough to confine himself to matters immediately pertaining to his defence,' the Judge of the Nottingham Crown Court interjected harshly.

'This trifling irregularity aside, comrade, I humbly submit that all my efforts were on behalf of England. If I may address myself to my friends of the media in the gallery, I would only add that this is a strange quirk of justice that finds the saviour of England in a felon's dock when by rights he should be in the courtyard of Buckingham Palace as recipient of honours from Her Majesty, because without wishing to boast unduly, your honour, I am the man who saved your bloody bacon in the Fourth Test.'

'Clear the galleries of all newspaper people,' the presiding judge commanded. 'However before they are evicted I would remind them that the prisoner's foregoing statement has been struck from the court records, meaning that any attempt to publish or broadcast his statement, in whole or in part, will be instantly punishable by the impounding of the presses, imprisonment, transportation or the severing of the offending hand. Pray continue, Peat.'

'I wish to call a new witness!' England's former umpire bellowed.

The Judge adjusted his pince-nez and looked down at the dock with an expression of forbidding austerity.

'The prisoner has been offered ample opportunity to call witnesses, is that not correct Mr Jardine?' The pince-nez gleamed in the direction of the young counsel for the defence.

'Correct your honour.'

'And as far as I am aware none has come forward.'

'Absolutely nobody your honour.'

'Then I rule the prisoner in contempt of court and. . . .'

'I call Mr James Ball of MI5 or MI6 – one of your secret Johnnies anyhow,' Reg Peat loudly appealed. 'Because he was the comedian who put me up to this. Said my country needed me. Said there would be a substantial career benefit in it. Not to mention an all-expenses-paid mini-break for three in the Seychelles! Send for James Ball, your lordship. He's the bastard who by rights should be standing here!'

A hammering gavel finally drowned the prisoner's words.

'Clerks, you will strike these statements from the records and ensure that they are shredded. The prisoner has mentioned a member of the Security Services by name. He is in the gravest possible contempt. Peat, have you anything more to say in your defence which is not likely to increase the further penalties that will be imposed upon you?'

'Only this your honour.' Had there been any reporters left in the court they would have noticed that a tear was gleaming on the veteran umpire's cheek. 'I've stood in quite a few places in my professional life. I've stood at Lord's and Edgbaston, Old Trafford and the Oval; I've stood in the damp of Hove and the heat of Canterbury and some other parts it would be improper to mention. I withstood the howls of the Swansea rabble, the vile imprecations of Headingley's hooligans. I've stood in fair and foul weather and give or take a few over-hasty decisions that fall to any umpire's lot, I like to think I've always stood for probity. There's only one place I've never stood, your excellency, and that is in the dock of a criminal courtroom. Can't you imagine the shame this is bringing on my family and lady acquaintances? Can't you find it in your heart to perceive, comrade, that this is punishment enough? Oh don't I know how tempting it is to raise an impetuous finger and thereby put a close to innings of rich promise. But look again at the man who is standing before you and make the prudent decision, your lordship, that he has already stood enough!'

The Judge of the Nottingham Crown Court appeared not to be listening to this impassioned address. He was busy smoothing a black handkerchief onto his grey wig.

There followed a resonant clearing of the throat. 'Let me recapitulate the charges on which the jury have found you guilty, overlooking, if we may, their quite wrong-headed recommendation for a degree of clemency. Peat, you have been found guilty of maliciously tampering with a light meter belonging to the Nottingham County Cricket Club. You have further been found guilty of grievous damage to the Trent Bridge tarpaulin covers and, by stealth, of watering with a corrosive substance a Test Match cricket pitch, again belonging to the Nottingham County Cricket Club.

'You have been accused, and you have offered no satisfactory defence, of seeking to offer visiting sportsmen to this country, who have a right to expect every showing of fair play and hospitality, alcoholic refreshments of the most dubious order. On the further charge of having locked the Australian tourists in their dressing room and having thrown away a key, which was again the property of the Nottingham County Cricket Club, you have been found unhesitatingly *guilty*. I will not dwell on the other time-wasting stratagems adopted by yourself at the aforesaid County Cricket ground since they are not actually punishable by law. But I am bound to rule that by your contemptible efforts to implicate members of the Security Services in your crimes you have made yourself eligible for a further onerous sentence.'

'Let the court be upstanding!' an official intoned.

'Peat,' the learned judge continued, 'you occupy a position of special responsibility in society. You are meant to be an ornament to the noblest of games, a model to the world of British fair play. You have shown yourself, on the contrary, to be an individual of the basest metal, and for this reason I intend to make an example of you. It is with no personal satisfaction that I sentence you to five years imprisonment for the crimes you committed at Trent Bridge, Nottingham and a further five years for your slanderous remarks concerning members of the Security Services. The sentences are not to run concurrently. Take the prisoner down.'

Additional warders had now entered the dock and were pulling and shoving at the recalcitrant felon.

'I've given you a clean sheet for the Oval. Thanks to me you can save the bloody Ashes there! England oh England, what crimes are committed in thy name!'

The former umpire had finally been removed from the dock although a section of the bars was still retained in his grasp.

'Take him down,' the judge nevertheless commanded, 'and ensure that these hysterical remarks are excised from the records!'

28

NEW APPOINTMENTS

In the first week of August, L. M. S. Partridge wrote to the Prime Minister to inform her that for reasons of health and pressure of his merchant banking interests he felt obliged to lay down the burden of Chairman of the England Selectors. The Prime Minister's office accepted his resignation with formal reluctance but pointed out that his letter should, rightfully, have been addressed to the Test and County Cricket Board, the authority still nominally responsible for the administration of the summer game.

At an extraordinary meeting in Downing Street, the Board immediately endorsed a new panel of selectors. Chaired by A.V. Bedser, formerly of Surrey, it represented an impressive pooling of mature selectorial skills. These included Mr P. B. H. May, Mr G. O. B. Allen and H. Elliot, the former Test umpire and Derbyshire player.

The new panel made sweeping changes to the England party for the Fifth Test at Kennington Oval. In contrast to the previous Chairman's policy of backing youth and innovation, Alec Bedser and his colleagues voted firmly for experience and a proven Test record. These were the names that were released to an expectant England on Sunday morning, 12 August.

J. M. Brearley (capt)
G. Boycott
M. C. Cowdrey

D. B. Close
E. R. Dexter
I. T. Botham
R. Illingworth
A. P. E. Knott (wkt)
J. C. Laker
J. A. Snow
R. G. D. Willis
R. D. Jackman

'At last we have a team that could stop the rot,' James Ball decided as he walked stiffly to the TV set to pressure into darkness a lunchtime news announcer about to turn to developments in the Middle East, Northern Ireland and the industrial scene. 'A little short of mobility in the field perhaps; but certainly the ability is there. And so are the brains, thank God. Young Brearley's grey cells are always worth two extra players to England.

'And this time, Buster,' he smiled as he moved slowly towards an Adam cabinet for a second gin and tonic, 'this time we need expect no interference from alien sources. We can look forward to the first true Test Match of the summer. We have a favourable response from T. G. K. Yellowfield.'

With an air of quiet satisfaction, if not of actual triumph, he slid two pieces of paper across his Georgian coffee table.

The first sheet was a photocopy of a letter addressed to the Secretary of the MCC. It read as follows:

Dear Mr Spriggs,

I was delighted to get your letter, and really quite touched that you and your Committee should have thought of me. Naturally I accept the captaincy of your forthcoming MCC tour with pleasure.

I have made enquiries about the constitution of the touring party and I am bound to confess I am a little concerned about the strength of the batting. Could not a few dependable middle-order batsmen like Joe Hardstaff, Denis Compton or

Maurice Leyland, if he's still available, be persuaded to turn out?

Please give it a thought. Meanwhile I am getting out my pads – dubbin is deuced hard to find in this Philistine city – and working on my field placings.

Yours appreciatively,
T. G. K. Yellowfield

PS The enclosed is for James Ball whose hand I suspect may have been behind your PS.

The second sheet of paper was the original of this note. Marked 'strictly confidential' it read as follows:

Dear Old Bally,

I got your message. Well it was you, wasn't it? Even in surrender, you've always been a rough old negotiator.

Frankly, my dear old antagonist, I'm so thrilled with my appointment to captain MCC against the might of Holland and Denmark, I'm quite prepared to accede to your cheese-paring demands.

Accordingly I've instructed Evelyn Lilliwhite to round up my agents in the field. It could get him back into the good books of the powers that be. And anyway I owe you a few agents.

I would be grateful if agent Stephanie could be returned more or less unharmed; but you can keep I. Smirnov if you want him. That boring old hillbilly never did understand the first thing about cricket anyway.

Perhaps we'll have occasion to meet over a bottle of Bols during the First Test at The Hague. In any case I'm glad I've made my point and you've had the nous to recognize it.

Love and kisses to Jan of course,
T.G.K.Y.

Buster Tolchard read both letters with care, then he laid them back on the Georgian coffee table and spoke.

'I'm a simple man, Bally, I mean Sir, I don't quite understand all the sophisticated things you've been getting up to, but I think I get the drift. From what I've heard of the young lady, I don't think I could trust myself with agent Stephanie; but I'd give my right arm to get the loathsome little greasepot, I. Smirnov in "the cage" at Harpenden. May I have your permission to run him in?'

'Why don't you pour yourself another cider and leave it to the "Oval",' his boss replied. 'Your energies could be needed later in the season, Buster, at "Checkpoint Charlie".'

29

ENGLAND STRIKES BACK

Agent Stephanie was arrested in Esher post office in the act of enquiring into the address and telephone number of Mr A. V. Bedser, the new Chairman of the England Selectors. She was ushered courteously into a Daimler by an MI5 man who then joined her in the back seat and nodded to the chauffeur with the word 'Heathrow'.

'Or perhaps you'd like to call round and collect your things first?' he added, 'although I'm afraid we couldn't let you take any guns out of the country.'

'I have nothing. As you can see,' Stephanie arched a bare leg upwards, 'I am practically naked.'

'We're going to put you on the 1.15 to Moscow if that's all right,' the secret service man said. 'I've got your ticket here. I'm afraid it's not a return.'

'Moscow is so boring in August,' she drawled. 'I would much prefer, if you please, the Dolomites. The air is so clean and fresh in those mountains. The fields are still a tapestry of beautiful wild flowers. I love to lie down in those sweet fields, just as I am, and let the scent of those flowers caress me.'

'I'm afraid this ticket is only for Moscow; but I dare say you could pick up a connecting flight there.'

'I have a good friend who lends me in the summer his chalet in the Dolomites. It is not so much a chalet, more a little castle with a dear old man and his wife who wait upon me hand and feet.' Her fingers played silent Alpine music on the MI5 man's knee. 'You could be my guest in this chalet,' she suggested in a silken whisper. 'We could be so happy, happy as two children at play, up there in the clouds.'

'To be honest I don't have a very good head for heights.'

'No? That is surprising because I see from your tie you are an Old Malvernian. You have there, do you not, those beautiful hills? Oh you know it is so wrong to be imprisoned in a Soviet airplane on a day like this. I feel I would like only to be wandering on those beautiful Malvern Hills. And you know you could take my hand,' she urged as she gently stroked her escort's shirt front, 'you could take my hand and then in the gloaming show me your old school, Roger, that is your name? I have a feeling it is.'

'Actually, my name is Nigel,' the MI5 man confessed, 'and incidentally, I think you ought to know I'm gay.'

'To be perfectly honest I don't care how many baths I am supposed to have taken with future cabinet ministers,' Sir Evelyn Lilliwhite hissed down the line. 'To be even franker, Mr Smirnov, I've had quite enough of you and your tiresome games. I'll thank you not to bother me again.'

'Then,' I. Smirnov answered with a sigh, 'you are leaving me no alternative but to leak these details to your gutter newspapers.'

'And I've got news for you, sweetie,' the MI5 director savaged back. 'I'm just signing a warrant for your arrest. I'll tell you another thing, I'm advising the Metropolitan Police to do it with maximum firepower, because it's quite obvious you're an armed lunatic. To be quite candid, my seedy little Slav, you'll be lucky if you even get to "the cage" in Harpenden in one piece!'

'You cannot arrest me. That is the agreement.'

'Oh yes I can, baby. And with the full authority of General Tristan Field himself – namely your boss! Oh you've really put your foot in it with him, I can tell you. He's given me carte blanche to rub you out, because he can't stand your oafish, peasant manners any more than I can.'

'You must listen to me please,' I. Smirnov stammered, for he was genuinely taken aback.

'If I were you, little man, I would get off my private line fast. You're probably already surrounded by sharpshooters.'

'But hear me please . . . my mission is not completed. There is still remaining the vital Fifth Test Match.'

'Are you talking about cricket again you boring little man? Let me tell you I've heard quite enough about that deadly game for one summer. To be perfectly honest, I can't wait for the football season – at least those pimply hooligans don't interfere with my music programmes. No wonder you've bored them to distraction in Moscow. As far as we're concerned you and your loathsome cricket can get blowed.'

The line fell noisily silent.

I. Smirnov replaced the receiver and walked rapidly from the lounge of his West Kensington hotel without pausing to check out. In the street he started, instinctively, to run. He ran for five blocks until shortage of breath and reason prevailed. He was only wasting energies it was essential to preserve, he reflected; besides by running in a London street, without the appropriate athletic gear, he was drawing attention to himself.

He limped into a Westbourne Terrace public house and ordered half a Watney's special with a vodka chaser. The effect was not entirely restorative. Confused images of terror and punishment danced before his eyes. The muzzles of the Metropolitan Police, 'the cage' in Harpenden, the bleak undulations of the Sino-Russian border, the cellars of the Lubianka.

He ordered a straight vodka this time, and considered again the implications of his recent telephone conversation with the MI5 mole. The truth of the matter was that he had been badly jolted by Sir Evelyn's sudden switch from reluctant patronage to spiteful hostility. This and the problems of language and nuance were obstacles to a cool appraisal of the situation. There could be no doubt that he had fallen seriously out of favour in Moscow. Worse, that he had incurred the displeasure of the most dreaded name in the KGB hierarchy. But the exact cause of his unpopularity was unclear. Was his fault too much diligence or too little? Perhaps that loathsome agent, Stephanie, had reported him, as she had hinted she might, for adopting over-drastic methods. On the other hand, out of professional jealousy, it was equally possible that she had informed on him for lack of ruthlessness.

Certainly Lilliwhite was the mouthpiece of Moscow, and somewhere among his irritable and garbled sentences, Smirnov reasoned, must lie the precise wishes of his employers. The last irritated explosion of the supermole seemed on deeper reflection to provide a clue. 'They can't wait for the football season,' wasn't that what Moscow's servant had reported? 'And all the time you do nothing else but talk. You're boring them to distraction in Moscow, you pimply little football hooligan. Why don't you blow that loathsome game of cricket up!'

The weight of the evidence seemed to point towards action, action of the most conclusive and drastic kind. Only a dramatic outrage against the game he had undertaken to destroy appeared to offer hope of a return to favour.

I. Smirnov slid from the bar stool and walked over to a cubicle of frosted glass which contained the tavern's pay telephone. There he dialled a certain Middle Eastern agency with which he had established contacts.

'This is agent I. Smirnov,' he spoke softly into the mouth-piece. 'I wish to speak with your most reliable demolitions expert.'

30

THE ULTIMATE TEST

'I really don't know what came over me,' Hector Bootle confessed as he drove in a taxi with James Ball towards Vauxhall Bridge and the Oval. 'They say it's something that happens to all of us in early middle age; but you wouldn't remember about that, I suppose. She was a damned attractive little minx of course; but the worrying thing is I seem to have gone absolutely barking bonkers about her. Still it's all over now. Sent her packing, didn't we?'

'Some of us did,' Ball corrected him gently.

'Anyway I sent that damned croquet set back to Fortnum & Mason. No, all things considered, we've come out of it with surprisingly few scars. The PM has been remarkably understanding. Says this kind of thing often happens with her younger ministers. Seems I've avoided the main pitfall which is begetting a love child. No, my chief worry now is how you've been managing, James, while I've been so to speak "indisposed". I have to admit to a certain feeling of unease.'

Between the South Bank office buildings, Ball caught a glimpse of gasometers, and experienced a whiff of the swelling anticipation he had felt as a schoolboy, hurrying Ovalwards to Hobbs and Sandham.

'I think we're entitled to enjoy a day's cricket,' he said. 'And at last we really do have a representative England team.'

'What worries me, James, is that we still haven't put I. Smirnov in the bag – or rather you haven't. I appreciate you've been a bit overworked recently, but I'm not sure if in your place I'd have left the job to Lilliwhite's boys.'

'It looks like a good day for winning the toss,' Ball observed. He added, 'I'd be very surprised if friend Smirnov shows up. He not exactly persona grata with anyone at the moment.'

'I'll tell you one thing about my brief sabbatical, James, it's given me a chance to relax the mind, get the old mental juices flowing again, brush up on perspective and that precious commodity we all need in this business – instinct. Now one thing my instinct is telling me, James, is that you're falling back into that dangerous complacency of yours. All right, you've done a deal with that blackguard Field. I'm not going to criticize that decision because I wasn't available to question it at the time. But I am thinking, and remember that I'm thinking pretty clearly now, that it's wide-eyed in the extreme to take that cheating swine at his word.'

'I'm glad I've kept my Surrey membership,' Ball mused, 'it means that we can sit in the pavilion. It's a funny thing, you know, I still get a kind of thrill from brushing sleeves with a Test batsman on his way to the middle.'

'You see, you're making my point for me, James. You will take your eye off the ball when there's no one to stand over you and din into your head the absolute neccessity of vigilance at all times.'

'We're here,' James announced with a childlike smile. 'If you'll get the cushions I'll get the scorecards. We've just got time to settle in before the players come out.'

As the two men went through the turnstile by the Hobbs Gate, a dark, thickset man with rolled up shirt sleeves was hurrying out. He pushed through the approaching crowds and came to a panting stop by a man reading an early edition of the *Standard* at the entrance of the Oval tube station.

'That a big place you want to blow,' he whistled for breath. 'That not so easy as an air terminal. Don't worry I pack it good. I got plastic all round the stadium. I got it on the roofs, I got it under the seats, I got it in all the latrines. And in the basement over there, yes that's right the pavilion, I got a ton of TNT.'

I. Smirnov surfaced from the *Standard* with a questioning expression.

'I asked please only for a detonation on the wicket.'

'Don't worry,' his new associate, Shamak, panted. 'That blow too. Everything in there blow good. You will see.'

The thickset man noticed signs of nervousness on his Russian colleague's part.

'It's all right.' He pulled him back from the escalators of the Oval underground station. 'No bang yet. See this little calculator? This way I activate. But not yet. First we telephone with the demand. Scare them good.'

'Please what demand?' Smirnov enquired with a troubled grin.

'Instant release of all prisoners in Israel and Imperialist gaols, restoration of West Bank to Palestine peoples, resignation of US puppet Egyptian government, abdication of Jewish financed Moroccan monarchy, liberation of North Ireland, total surrender of Iraqi jackals to Iranian freedom forces!'

'I asked only for an outrage. I wished to make no demands,' I. Smirnov protested.

'You crazy? You gotta to have demands.' Shamak mildly shook the smaller man. 'Otherwise that's like a terrorist. That's not like freedom fighter. I am freedom fighter,' he emphasized with a tightening grip on I. Smirnov's lapel. 'You got to have demands – big demands. Anyway we make them sweat, you see. 'Cause I fix the detonator smart. They never going to find it!'

'It's been a very encouraging morning's play, hasn't it Richie, for England that is?' Peter West beamed into camera. 'Of course we had that early upset when we lost Brearley cheaply. But that, if anything, is going to make him even more determined to mastermind another England victory. Here's his dismissal coming up on our screen now. Your comments, Tom. But meanwhile we've had this very impressive stand between Boycott and Cowdrey and I must say, I don't know what you think Richie, it's taken one right back to the seventies or even the late sixties – two of the great figures of postwar Test history really knuckling down to it and showing, perhaps for the first time in this series, that England is a force to be reckoned with!

'You're right, Richie, it hasn't been a run feast; but the point is that both these great England stalwarts are *not out* at lunch. And they have been prepared to hit the occasional loose ball, haven't they Tom? You remember when Geoff Boycott let go at that long hop from Terry Alderman after the drinks interval. Here it is coming up on our screen now. You see. He's giving it a pretty convincing clip, and it's nearly a four. But the point is, isn't it Richie, that England are 53 for one wicket – just that of Mike Brearley dismissed early – at lunchtime. And that's the solidest England start we've seen for a long time.'

The early afternoon was a treat for England supporters. The unfortunate running out of Colin Cowdrey just after the resumption had the compensation of bringing Dexter to the wicket. After an uncertain start, the former England captain was soon launched into strokes calculated to stir memories of distant sixties' summers. While Hector Bootle tucked into a crab salad and sipped at a bottle of Chablis from his portable freezer, James Ball chewed contentedly on a pork pie. The afternoon seemed to stretch in front of him like a pleasurable eternity. Ahead lay sweet hours of stroke-making and run-stealing, and if this was not sustenance enough, there was always that extra bar of Cadbury's milk chocolate in his picnic box.

England was moving ahead confidently now. So much so that even the dismissal of Boycott seemed a tolerable misfortune. Close's dismissal was cause for mild concern; but it made way for an aggressive Botham. The two most attacking England batsmen of the postwar era were joined in an exciting partnership, the younger man inspiring a competitive hostility in the lordly batsman who had once put Hall and Griffith to the sword.

Only one thing seemed to mar this delectable partnership and that was the increasing number of police and army personnel who were moving about among the seats, obscuring the view of vintage drives and hooks. Then the day-dreaming afternoon was shattered like a clap of thunder. A pluck at the sleeve. An army sergeant saluting. 'Compliments of Major Woodvine, Sir. Would you and Mr Bootle be good enough to report to the Secretary's office.'

A tense group was waiting for them in the Secretary's office. Beside the chain-smoking Surrey Secretary stood a major of the Royal Engineers thrashing at his camouflage trousers with a cane. In the background was the debonair but pale figure of the Commissioner of the Metropolitan Police.

'I'm glad both of you are at the Test today,' the Secretary said when he had effected his introductions. 'The point is that we've had a telephone call from a group calling itself World Liberation.'

'If we don't accede to their demands, in four minutes twenty seconds,' the Major explained, 'they're going to activate a mechanism which will make the Oval as lethal as an ammunition dump in a forest fire.'

'The trouble is,' the Surrey Secretary took up the story, 'their demands are almost impossible to meet. I mean we're frankly in no position here to secure the release of every prisoner in Israeli gaols; let alone engineer the downfall of the Moroccan monarchy.'

'I told you to beware complacency, didn't I James!' Hector Bootle exclaimed.

'My chaps have managed to remove a fair amount of a highly combustible material from various of the stands,' Major Woodvine of the bomb-disposal squad continued in calm but not altogether reassuring tones. 'I've got to hand it to to these Johnnies, though. They've set us one hell of a puzzle. You pull out a lump of plastic here. Disconnect a circuit there. But you don't seem to get at their main system.'

'Of course we're in direct telephone contact with the Prime Minister,' said the Commissioner of the Metropolitan Police.

'But frankly even she can't be expected to secure the return of the West Bank in an afternoon,' the Surrey Secretary pointed out as he lit another cigarette.

'You see the result, James, of taking your eye off the ball,' Hector Bootle scolded.

'We've only got one thing to go on,' Major Woodvine said. 'The fellow who rang up with his demands seems remarkably pleased with his detonator system. Could we hear the replay again please, Commissioner.'

The senior police official pressed a small tape recorder on the Secretary's desk. A foreign voice spoke excitedly from the machine.

' . . . hey and you never find that detonator because this one is real smart. You never guess where. And at sixteen hours prompt I activate it by remote control. It only going to need a little tap to blow you good!'

The Major raised his binoculars and began another visual search of the crowded cricket ground. 'Somewhere out there, if we only knew where, is the trigger to this whole fiendish system. Oh my God!'

Four other binoculars levelled on the Oval pitch.

'There! At the further wicket,' the Major indicated with a gasp. 'What a hideously cunning device!'

The bowler had paused to do up his bootlaces. Botham, the facing batsman, was in an amiable conversation with the wicket keeper. But it was to the wicket itself that the Major directed Ball's glasses. At first he noticed nothing unusual, and then he saw it – a hairline-thin length of yellow wire running down the side of the middle stump.

'The blighter's even fixed it so that any stump can detonate us,' the Major spoke through a closed jaw.

James twiddled at his eyepiece for clearer vision. Sure enough, he saw that the stumps were connected by cobweb-thin wires.

'Gentlemen, it is four p.m. precisely,' the Commissioner of the Metropolitan Police announced. 'The device is now activated.'

At this moment, Botham heaved for another six and was

caught on the long on boundary.

'Who is the next man in?' Major Woodvine huskily enquired. 'He'll need to be the best batsman in England.'

'I think it's Alan Knott,' the Surrey Secretary replied. 'He's always been a sprightly little run-maker, but he does chance his arm a bit.'

'We need a Boycott in there while we find out how to defuse this hellish thing!' cried the Major.

'Unfortunately Boycott is out,' the Secretary reminded him.

'It's Knott all right,' said Ball.

'You're telling me it's not all right!' Hector Bootle thundered. 'It's a bloody fiasco and all because of that dangerous complacency of yours James! Look, get that man in here. We can't risk a cricketer of his class in a situation like this!'

At the window of the Secretary's office Alan Knott, helmeted and padded, was waving cheerily to the Surrey official, preparatory to his walk to the wicket.

'What do you propose?' the Surrey Secretary wondered as he drew the great Kent player into the crisis meeting.

'Major, how long do you need?' Bootle turned to the military expert.

'There's a tea interval coming up at four-ten, isn't there? If someone could hold out there for ten minutes that would give us nearly half an hour to locate the lead from that wicket.'

'So, someone's got to go out there and stay in for ten minutes.' Bootle's bulging gaze moved from the Surrey Secretary to the Commissioner of Police and finally came to rest on James.

'Would it not be a sensible idea, in the circumstances, to advance the tea interval by ten minutes,' Ball mildly suggested.

'A special announcement to the effect that tea will be taken early while the army defuses an explosive device?' the Secretary pondered. 'There are a lot of people in the ground this afternoon. It could cause a certain amount of panic.'

'Of course it would cause a panic!' Hector Bootle bellowed. 'People would be fighting to get out, walking all over each other – trampling on babies! It would be bloody mayhem out there.

No, someone's got to pad up and get out there and take it on the jaw. Has anyone amongst us four any experience of first-class cricket?'

There was a silence.

Again Bootle's gaze came to rest on Ball. 'James, you played for Cambridge didn't you?'

'And what a pleasure it is to see Alan Knott in an England cap, or rather an England helmet, walking to the wicket in a Test Match for England again,' Tony Lewis exulted. 'Here comes that inimitable elfin figure wearing those outsize pads which have nevertheless seen him and England through many crises. And here again is that funny little stooping walk we've come to know so well over the years, if anything the stoop is a little more pronounced; but then I suppose, Trevor, it's a long time since we've seen Knotty in a Test Match.'

'It is a long time, Tony, and you're right. Alan Knott is looking a little older since we last saw him in a Test Match.'

'He's looking a sight older since I saw him last week,' Freddie Trueman observed.

And yet, as he took guard, James Ball felt as cold in his bowels as a schoolboy in his first house match. The difference was that then he had been able to see the umpire clearly. Now, with his spectacles in the breast pocket of his pin-stripe back in the pavilion, he could discern only a white blur.

Had he really played for Cambridge? Had he really bowled the Nawab of Pataudi? And on the previous day helped Radcliffe to a famous century? It had been so long ago and age could play tricks with even the most fastidious memories. Was the truth perhaps that the University had given him a trial against a county like Leicestershire and Northants and the honour had expanded in his mind to a varsity match cap? The truth, in any case, was irrelevant now. As far as Hector Bootle had been concerned, he had played for Cambridge at Lord's. And now he was batting for England in a Test Match against Australia with the fate of thousands depending on his defence of his wicket.

He was still engaged on these thoughts when he heard a whistling sound like an artillery shell and realized that he had received his first ball from Jeff Thomson. The thump of the ball impacting with the wicketkeeper's gloves told him it had missed.

He peered down the wicket. Beyond the blur of the umpire he could see the smaller white speck of the bowler. It was growing rapidly in size. But when exactly would it reach the wicket and when would it release the ball? This business of deception was all very well, James bleakly reflected; but he should have insisted on wearing his spectacles to the wicket. It was an academic thought because now he was reeling from a rocket strike on his helmet. Thomson had tried him with a short one. The bat slipped from his hands. He opened his eyes and saw blue sky. He was falling, falling backwards onto the wicket. Voices burbled in his subconscious 'dangerous complacency James' . . . 'you will take your eye off the ball' . . . 'don't seem to be able to get at the main system' . . . 'It only going to need a little tap to blow you good!' It was these last few words spoken in an excitable foreign accent that alerted the half-concussed ex-civil servant to the horrendous danger. He could not break his fall; but he could perhaps shift its direction. He hit the ground only inches from the baited stumps.

Slip fielders raised him to his feet with few expressions of sympathy. Did someone murmur 'Pommie bastard'? Well this *was* a Test Match James reminded himself.

Just two more balls to face this over. Correction just one now. Thomson had released another rocket, seemingly without any warning. And now it was speeding towards deep third man by way of his dangling bat.

'Come on!' shouted Tex Dexter halfway down the wicket.

The temptation to obey his call was almost overwhelming. The first run he had ever made in Test cricket (and possibly his last) was there for the taking. Moreover Ted Dexter was now three-quarters way down the pitch.

'Stay!' James commanded with a raised glove. He had made a solemn undertaking back in the Secretary's office that he would hold his end up until tea time. He could not go back on that undertaking now.

A puzzled Dexter only just managed to regain his crease. Now there remained but one ball to the over. Again the whistle of a descending shell. Now behind him a deafening appeal.

The white blur of the umpire seemed to be unmoved. 'Not out,' he added on further raucous enquiry. A correct decision in James's view. He had never seen the ball.

Dexter now faced. He hit two fours and then called Ball for a single which the latter sternly refused. They ran two for the next stroke. Then Dexter summoned a mid-wicket conference.

'Knotty, you don't look too happy with Thomson. I've got my eye in, why don't you let me see him out till tea time? I'll take a single off the next ball and you can play yourself in at this end. By the way are you feeling all right? You look dreadful.'

James Ball was not a natural impersonator. To have spoken would have given the desperate game away. So he merely nodded ambiguously. However when Dexter called for a single he again sent him back with a firm 'Stay!', although his heart and intestines were gripped by dread.

'And now it's Thomson to bowl again to Alan Knott. I should think that what's in the back of his mind – I don't know about you Freddie – is that if he can get one under Alan's bat before the tea interval, then the picture for England won't be as rosy as it looked earlier.'

'And 'e's been showing every sign of doing that Brian. I've frankly never seen Knotty look so uncomfortable against pace.'

'All the same, Freddie, if he can last this over which looks like being the last over before tea, he'll no doubt feel a lot better when he's got a good warm cuppa inside him and a slice or two of fruit cake.'

'There can be no doubt,' Trevor Bailey interjected, 'that, for the time being at any rate, Alan Knott is struggling to find his touch. That one shaved his off stump by a whisker.'

'Close your eyes and think of England.' No, the sage old

housemaster's homily was inappropriate to this moment, James Ball decided. But the recall of those wise old words had released another memory from the housemaster's long dead fireside, another prescription for the game of life which seemed to have a special validity now. 'Wherever you go, whatever you do when you leave school, you will find no sterner examiner than the batting crease.'

Recalling those words afresh at this Oval Test crease, they seemed to have contained an element of personal prophecy. He had been to a few places in the world, not infrequently with the travelling companion of danger. He had also achieved a little in his lifetime – some of the things he had done since he left school were matters for quiet satisfaction. That first in classics from Cambridge, for instance. Ball had even supposed that the sternest tests in life were behind him. But his old housemaster, as always, had known better. The supreme trial had still been waiting for him. The ultimate test was here and now!

In this mood of strengthened resolve, Ball prepared to face the next delivery from Thomson. At least that was the name on the scorecard. Ball could only see an approaching white blur. Who was to say he was not shaping up to an even more formidable identity? As the white figure neared the popping crease, Ball could hear a rushing as if of angel's wings. Was it too irrational to believe it was Gabriel, not Thomson who was bearing down on him? Or even the supreme examiner himself?

'Who would true valour see, let him come hither!' It was, to the words of a school chapel hymn ringing in his ears that Ball danced down the wicket and sliced the ball high over slips heads for four runs.

'For heaven's sake keep your eye on the ball, James!' Hector Bootle hollered from the pavilion. 'Your job is to stay there!'

James did not hear him. He listened for the scream of the ball he no longer had eyes to see, and swatted at it as if at a wasp. Three runs to the legside here. But no. Dexter must not be risked at the batting crease. 'Just two will do,' he panted as he staggered back into his end.

There had been method in his seeming madness. The show

of aggression was bound to sting the Queenslander into retaliation – in other words a bumper which, if he could avoid it, would be certain to clear the lethal stumps. In fact, Thomson bowled two bumpers. One cleared Ball's helmet by yards. The second removed it. Now James had reason to be grateful for his schooling in the slips. He spun round and caught the falling helmet a fraction of a second before it hit the bails and blew Kennington Oval into the skies.

One more ball to survive. He did not need to see the expression on the demon or divine bowler's face to know this would be the most testing of all. Somehow he made contact with a screaming yorker. But the force of the thing could not be muzzled by a drop of the wrists. Even Horatius' sword must have begun to feel fragile against the increasing weight of all Tuscany. It was the same with Ball's bat. Slowly but inexorably it was being pressured back out of the block hole by the sheer energy of the ball he had met with a full blade.

Time goes into slow motion at moments like these. James could see the ball rolling onwards towards the stumps, and was fully aware that there was nothing in the rules to prevent him from kicking it away. It impacted with the stumps as James's boot was still raised to deliver the saving kick.

'What a grand little entertainer this man Knotty still is!' Tony Lewis exulted. 'He's lying flat on the wicket with his hands to his ears or, I should say, to his helmet, as if to say I really made a balls or, I should say, a mess, of that one. But the tragedy is that the defences of this plucky little fighter have been penetrated. There are the bails coming off now . . . . '

For some time Ball lay on the Oval wicket as his wartime firewatching service had taught him. Stomach and face hugging the earth to present the lowest possible silhouette to blast, hands on ears to obviate damage to the hearing.

It was only the megaphone tones of Hector Bootle which finally got through to him, 'For God's sake get up James, we've got it under control now!'

As Ball rose slowly to his feet, dusting the Oval sand off Alan Knott's white trousers, he was dimly aware of a waving khaki figure on the steps of the pavilion. He could not see the loops of severed wire the Major was clutching in his triumphant hand, nor understand, as he would come to learn later, that the lead from the detonator/wicket had been discovered and cut only seconds before he had been finally bowled.

'No ball,' the umpire called on reflection.

James Ball was still being helped to his feet when the last delivery of the over burst through the Australian wicketkeeper's clutching glove for four byes.

Not before time, the umpires removed the bails for the tea interval.

31
CLOSE OF PLAY

It was the morning after England won the Fifth Test Match at the Oval to square the series, and retain the Ashes.

James Ball set down his suitcase in the hall and called up to his wife. 'I'm just popping out for a moment.' An official limousine was waiting for him in the street. It drove him to Heathrow where, without the normal security formalities, he boarded a British Airways flight to Berlin, Tempelhof.

The copy of the morning *Times*, handed to him by a simpering stewardess, contained encouraging news. On page one it was reported that as a result of a dynamic initiative from the Home Secretary, a notorious Russian agent named Ike Molotov and his Third-World accomplice had been run to ground by units of the Metropolitan Police and the Royal Engineers in the Surrey Tavern, Kennington.

'So that disposes of friend Smirnov, at least for the time being,' Ball murmured over his plastic coffee cup.

But the big story was, of course, England's convincing victory in the Fifth Test Match. Ball lingered over Woodcock's full report. It paid handsome tributes to the Selectors for their courage in backing experience, and it was fulsome in its praises of Michael Brearley's tactical acumen. Boycott, Dexter and Botham were applauded for their contributions to England's impressive first innings total. But the highest laurels were reserved for Alan Knott. '. . . coming in when the innings was still in the balance,' wrote the doyen of cricket reporters, 'Knott at first encountered difficulty in re-acclimatizing himself to the demands of cricket at Test Match level. However he stuck to his task with commendable courage and resilience and there can be no doubt that his innings of 105 contributed in no small measure to England's ultimate victory.'

'Correction,' Ball murmured into his complimentary gin and tonic. 'He scored precisely 99. Six of his runs were mine.'

Harry Grimaldi and his Pitch Rollers were waiting for him in a disused tool shed under the Berlin Wall.

'Everything in order, Harry?'

'No problems. We've got spotters out all along the wall, and one of our people over there will give us the wink as soon as things start to move.'

Ball gave the old freelance spytrapper a cool appraisal.

'What is this garment you're supposed to be wearing, Harry?'

'MCC blazer, isn't it? Well, you asked for a convincing looking welcoming committee didn't you, Bally?'

'Take it off and hide it,' Ball rapped out with sudden authority. 'That's a Middlesex supporter's blazer you're wearing. In any case, the MCC are wearing striped blazers abroad these days.'

'There's something happening over there now,' Buster Tolchard reported from his spy hole in the tool shed's bullet-ridden walls.

An official car flying the Hammer and Sickle flag had drawn up at the East German checkpoint. Ball snatched Grimaldi's binoculars and pressed them against a pair of bullet holes. He could smell him, but he could not see him. The car was surrounded by 'Kapos' and their restless Alsatians. 'Where is he?' he heard himself hiss.

Harry Grimaldi put a cricket-sweatered sleeve around his shoulder. 'Take it easy, Bally, I know you've got a personal interest in this, as well as the security one. Don't worry. We'll have him in "the cage" at Harpenden by tea time.'

'I don't know what you're talking about,' Ball coolly replied, although his heart was racing.

'They're raising the barrier. They're waving someone through. Here he comes; the swine!' Buster Tolchard reported with increasing excitement.

Ball slapped Grimaldi's binoculars back into the spy holes. A tall man was walking with a carefree gait directly towards their hideout. As he drew closer, Ball became surer that the invitation had been answered. The tall elderly figure was carrying an ancient leather cricket bag on which the initials T.G.K.Y. were clearly discernible. At the man's collar was an MCC tie, not the dull city version favoured by stockbrokers and insurance clerks, doubtful if their application for membership had actually been confirmed; but the flamboyant scarlet and gold tie of men who have truly put bat to ball for the greatest of all clubs.

'Come on baby, come on, my little darling!' Grimaldi urged under his breath. 'Come to daddy, come to Harry, come to "the cage" at Harpenden!'

He was close enough now for there to be no mistake. The intellectual's brow. The arrogant beak of a nose. It was Tristan Field without a shadow of doubt. Only the expression was new to Ball. He was wearing a smile of blissful happiness.

'All right, Harry, give him three more paces and step out and welcome him – on behalf of the MCC! No wait!'

As if from nowhere, a woman had sprung out in front of them into the no-man's land between East and West. Now she was waving frantically at the returning exile.

'Stop! Oh please stop!' they could hear her cry. 'You're walking into a trap.'

'I've got a Lee Enfield with a silencer,' Harry Grimaldi muttered. 'I can pick her off now if you want.'

'No. For God's sake no!' Ball gasped. The woman had turned her face to their hideout in order to indicate the threat to Field. Through Grimaldi's binoculars he had come face to face with his wife, Jan.

'She must have caught the 12.45 from Heathrow,' he added under his breath.

Now he saw Field hesitate and saw a terrible battle convulse the traitor's features. The brow and the nose were saying it was time to beat a retreat. The expanding nostrils were registering mortal danger. But in the grey eyes was a look of desperate longing. Ball knew instinctively what those eyes were seeing – the playing fields of Holland and Denmark and beyond them, perhaps, the forbidden plot of Lord's itself. Very reluctantly Tristan Field began to turn his back on the pleasure gardens of the West.

'Wait Tristan, you must take me with you!' the woman began to scream. 'Oh yes, my love, yes, there have been others I confess. But never, never, like you. I've been living a lie all these years Tristan. Whatever I've told Bally there is only you my lovely all-rounder!'

What happened next took everyone by surprise, including James. Suddenly he was out in no-man's land where the Kapos' sub-machine guns were beginning to spurt. For a second Jan was transfixed between them – a scowling uncertain Field, a husband whose patience had finally snapped. Then the balance shifted. Field was running back to the Wall and Jan was straddled across Ball's knee. The machine guns of East and West began a confused rattle; but the loudest smacks were to be felt on Jan Ball's bottom.

'Now we'll go home and you'll cook me dinner for once,' James told her masterfully. 'And by the way you can mend a hole in my homburg. It seems to have caught a communist bullet.'

'On the whole, Mr Ball,' said the Prime Minister, 'I understand you're to be congratulated, if not as a spycatcher at least as a batsman. I understand your effort at the Oval, for which, of course, you can never hope to receive any official recognition, was quite splendid.'

'Thank you Ma'am.'

'I gather you have also given considerable service to us in the arrest or deportation of the two minor agents Smirnov and Stephanie. My husband and I would like to express our thanks.'

'Thank you Ma'am.'

'We've also decided to act on your recommendation that it's time for a change at the top at the "Oval". What was the post you suggested might be suitable for Sir Evelyn Lilliwhite?'

'President of the MCC – for life.'

'Of course; but he tells me he loathes cricket.'

'Exactly Ma'am,' James answered with a sly grin.

'Ah yes, I see your point. The post could be suitable. I'm afraid the attempt to recapture Mr Tristan Field says less for your good judgement, doesn't it Mr Ball?'

'There were complications we could not have foreseen,' James answered flatly.

'On the other hand I suppose it can be argued he's had a pretty good fright. Perhaps this sleeping dog will really lie down from now on. Certainly his capture would have been bound to stir up all those Parliamentary questions again.'

'There is that point, Ma'am,' James agreed.

'On the whole, Mr Ball, I'm tempted to agree with Her Majesty that your service to us merited a knighthood such as we've been pleased to award to Sir Hector Bootle. Unfortunately the scandalous display by Mrs Ball on the Berlin Wall –and thank heavens no media reporters were there – has made that impossible. For this reason we are making you an offer of an OM which implies no particular merit on the part of the wife. What are you laughing about Mr Ball?'

A phrase spoken long ago at a housemaster's fireside had surfaced in Ball's mind, the same good man who had spoken of thinking of England with closed eyes and remembering that the crease was the sternest examiner. Although he had been revered for his high morals, this old housemaster, as Ball remembered now, had married a former model from south-east London whose behaviour was less widely respected. And yet he had been fiercely loyal to his unconventional spouse, and urged on his pupils a similar attitude, no matter whom they married on leaving the house.

'I was thinking of a homily I learned at school, Prime Minister,' James explained. 'You may say of my wife that that's no lady; but I say that lady is my wife!'

On the following pages are details of Arrow books that will be of interest.

SCORPION

- ★ A beautiful girl brutally abducted from the streets of Paris
- ★ The secret agent's corpse cast up on a beach – without arms or legs
- ★ A Saudi prince with perverted sexual tastes – and fanatic ambitions
- ★ The Moscow-bred plot to sever the Free World's most vital life line
- ★ A mystery assassin lured ever deeper into a lethal web of treachery

From the remote Beduin tents of Arabia to the secret conferences of the Western super-rich, a razor-edged thriller of explosive violence.

MONTE CARLO

Stephen Sheppard

It is May 1940 when Harry Pilikian, a young American, drives his Rolls Royce through the French night. By the time he reaches the principality of Monaco, the Germans have invaded France – and the war begins in earnest.

In neutral Monte Carlo, for the next two years, an uncertain peace prevails. The Italian army pays a token visit, Gestapo men move about in plain clothes, and refugees from all parts of the world – the rich, beautiful and bizarre – gather to sit out the war in safety and comfort.

But amidst the glitter and elegance of this famous resort, the menace of engulfing war is never far away. And those who fled to Monte Carlo for sanctuary are inescapably drawn into the anguish and horror of the conflict . . .

THE MANCHURIAN CANDIDATE

Richard Condon

To the Americans, Sergeant Raymond Shaw is a hero of the highest honours.

To the Russians, he is the most valuable assassin they could ever hope to have.

Captured by the communists in Korea, Sergeant Raymond Shaw has been secretly brain-washed and programmed. Now he will kill and kill on command; then have no memory of having killed, or even of having had the thought of killing. Thus he can feel no guilt. Feeling no guilt, he has no fear of being caught. And so, feeling neither hesitation, guilt, nor fear, Sergeant Raymond Shaw will always be a normal, sober, productive and even upstanding citizen – on the surface.

'Plausibility . . . pace . . . tremendously readable and convincing' Kingsley Amis, *Observer*

£1.75

HELL IS ALWAYS TODAY

Jack Higgins

'We're pretty hot on parking tickets, but not so good on maniacs who walk the streets on wet nights murdering women.'

Police morale is low. A callous, motiveless killer has the city in a stranglehold of fear as he casually selects his fifth victim. Even the whores are staying at home, and as public anxiety increases Mallory and Miller, the hard-pressed officers assigned to the case, realize their troubles are just beginning . . .

Not only a new corpse found in the driving rain, but, just to complicate matters, news of a dangerous criminal on the run.

MASTER OF THE MOOR

Ruth Rendell

There had been one victim found already, young and blonde, her face disfigured, her head shorn — killed without motive or mercy.

Now it was as though the ancient, treacherous moor had become the whole world, the dark and dangerous centre of everything. There were nearly fifty men on it, all searching with only one purpose, all summoned by one unknown man. One victim had already been found and now, because another woman was missing, they had come as though they were, in fact, his slaves . . .

'Excellent, macabre . . .' *The Spectator*

'Our leading lady 'whydunnit' writer' Graham Lord, *Sunday Express*

'A splendidly sinewy tale' H. R. F. Keating, *The Times*

£1.50